Dear Samuel Hahnemann,
thank you.
You found homeopathy.

Petra Neumayer is a well-known medical journalist and author in Europe. She has written many books about alternativ medicine which have been translated into seven languages. Her book "Healing with numbers" climbed to the Top-Twenty, making her a bestselling author. In 2013 her book „Painting the energy body" was published by Inner Traditions in the USA. Hahnemann's Legacy is her second novel. It takes a look at alternative medicine, the unknown world of homeopathy…

Petra Neumayer
Hahnemann's Legacy
®Skripthaus Verlag, Munich
Coverdesign: Thomas Blaha
Textdesign: Petra Neumayer
Editor: Lucia Eppelsheim
Translation: Lisa Rodgers
Print: Createspace
1st edition, April 2014
ISBN 978-1497589148

Visit the author at www.skripthaus.com

Petra Neumayer

Hahnemann's Legacy

Translated by Lisa Rodgers

Skripthaus Verlag

PROLOGUE

I don't know when you will be reading this; I may be dead already. Perhaps you would like to remember my name. I am called Hans Ganter.

Listen to this address by Samuel Hackman, Health Advisor to the city of New York, to begin with. It is a brief excerpt from a live television broadcast by New York station, ABC New York; a feature broadcast a few years after the death of Tinor MùMille.

Distinguished guests,

I cordially welcome all those present and those of you watching on television at home to our opening ceremony for the MùMille Memorial Hospital, in particular the clinic manager Dr. Nikola Milec and his deputy, Dr. Hans Ganter.

Tinor MùMille was one of the most prominent homeopathic practitioners of the modern era. An outstanding doctor who inherited the legacy of Hahnemann and, like him, wholly devoted himself to homeopathy. We thank this man for sacrificing his own life, in order to solely devote himself to homeopathic research. I call such outstanding healers, shadow healers, since on the one hand they practice their craft in

the shade of popular traditional medicine and because,
in reality, they are the only true healers; it is they who
heal the parts in us which have fallen into the shade, into
illness. With the MùMille Memorial Hospital we want to
cherish his memory and enable a large number of
patients to have access to the simple, yet ground-
breaking methods of homeopathic pulsation which he
developed.

At the celebrations to follow and as a sign of thanks
and of respect we would now like to hang portraits of Dr.
Tinor MùMille and of Dr. Friedrich Samuel Hahnemann
next to one another in the clinic foyer.

That the former New York Memorial Hospital has
been developed into a one-hundred-percent homeopathic
clinic – and that this has happened within such a short
time – ought certainly to be deemed a miracle! Spiritual
forces must have been at work to have pulled this off!
This new clinic should also be a symbol for us that a new
spiritual era has dawned!

To conclude, I call to the good of humanity, in
accordance with the homeopathic laws of healing, that
this may continue to spread across the entire globe.
Similia similibus curentur - Let like be cured by like!

Samuel Hackman, Health Advisor
for the city of New York

Can you imagine such a thing? A major American
city, riddled with debt, which did not know how to plug
the holes in its finances, suddenly allocated money – a
nine-digit amount – to turn a moribund city hospital in
need of renovation into a luxurious, alternative medicine

clinic; even though the signs of poverty and misery on the streets were more obviously crying out for help and for financial support? In a time when the struggle against terrorism engulfed all resources and thoughts? When the world was already in the process of destroying itself with terrorism and counter-terrorism?

But this was how it was; and that wasn't all. There was also the passion with which the doctors and nurses worked in this new clinic, me included. It was verging on devotion how attentively they treated their patients and how lovingly their little homeopathic dressings were applied; the amazingly successful healing which occurred in many of the patients within a short space of time was little short of a miracle. What I'm trying to say is that it was almost as if the entire clinic team had been vaccinated somehow or another, and as if it were the enthusiasm for homeopathy which was some sort of never-ending infection, transmitted to every person who worked in this clinic and to every person who was brought in as a patient.

I too loved my work above all else and it soon came to the point with me that I wanted to devote myself exclusively to homeopathic research, and so it was that I handed over my position as Deputy Clinic Manager to my successor, Dr. Carol Lewinsky. It was strange; Samuel Hahnemann and Tinor MùMille had also given up their practice work to wholly devote themselves to homeopathic research. To begin with it was thought that Hahnemann would then be plunged into destitution. Indeed, his sacrifice triggered an initiation for him, his spiritual awakening, and just two years later in 1790, he established homeopathy. Might it be better to say that he let God find him?

Yet I did not find much peace of mind for my research work, since the inner urge to find out more about the clinic founder, Dr. Tinor MùMille, always persisted. It wasn't just the fact that this increased day by day. I had learned about and worshipped this magnificent homeopathic practitioner during my time as a student, yet up until his death I actually knew nothing about his life.

One day I started to do some research and embarked on a search for the unassuming, modest traces which Tinor MùMille left behind. I even visited the most important places in his life, walked in his footsteps from Resina to Pompeii, questioned his surviving dependants and unearthed old newspaper articles about this wondrous man. With each new piece of information the fate of a genius and a maverick opened up before me; not only did I slowly and bit by bit begin to understand, during this biographical work it was at times even possible for me to completely immerse myself in Tinor MùMille's being; to think and to feel as he might have done. I pieced together the jigsaw and the result was an exceptional biography of a healer.

Chapter 1

"The physician's high and only mission is to restore the sick to health, to cure, as it is termed."
Samuel Hahnemann, Organon of Medicine. First appearance of the 6th edition, 1921

One of those heat waves, which would be talked about for years to come, had once again descended upon Southern Italy. For several days the temperatures soared to 45 degrees; even the wind at the sea seemed to abate. Many Southern Italian people remembered the summer of 1921, not just because of those sleepless, oppressive nights. Water was in short supply, and many elderly people suffered heatstroke. You could literally smell in the air that this heat would continue to weigh heavily and no change in the weather was to be expected any time soon. And where, centuries ago, Mount Vesuvius at the Gulf of Naples, unimpressed by human activity, blew its toxic gases into the night sky, Concetta was in labour and with one final, painful push, gave birth to her first son.

'Madonna! – That should be my boy!', cried the young mother, at the sight of the blood-smeared bundle which the old midwife placed into her arms. Concetta gazed, exhausted, at the crumpled, blue squishy mass which now lay wailing loudly in her arms, desperately searching for his mother's bosom to assuage his hunger. Yet Concetta refused this child her bosom. She had already given birth to six daughters and nourished them at her breast, but this was not her son! It was a sort of reluctance which suffused her upon sight of this new-born; almost choking her and taking her breath away.

She desperately wiped her hair, wet with sweat, out of her face. And at the thought of having to lie next to this child, that it would come even closer, new beads of sweat formed on her forehead and she had the feeling that something quite awful would happen. Concetta screamed out loudly and gesticulated wildly with her arms, as the brusque midwife tried again and again to lay the child at her breast. Even after several attempts the old lady did not succeed in ensuring that the child would be fed. There was nothing left for the midwife to do but take the blood-smeared bundle and hand it over to a wet-nurse for its first feed, until the young mother's hysteria had settled. Yet, with all the will in the world she could just not imagine that a normal person would become of this mass.

Even during pregnancy Concetta had harboured strange sentiments about the life growing within her belly. She would have preferred it if her husband Alfonso had not even noticed the pregnancy. Then she could have wrapped the child up in a woollen blanket right after it was born and placed it outside a church. Somebody would certainly have looked after it. Bartolo Longo perhaps. This church dignitary had seemingly nothing better to do than to gather up poor orphans from the streets. As if there were not any other misery which he could have been tending to!

Concetta would even have accepted a stillborn child, than breastfeed and bring up this son. In the beginning she had initially tried to conceal the pregnancy from Alfonso, yet Concetta, who was a small, petite Italian lady with an almost childlike physique - which she had kept even after six daughters - would not have been able to conceal the distinct bulge of her belly for long from her irascible husband.

Concetta also started to be stricken with vague anxieties during her pregnancy, accompanied and stirred by peculiar nightly dreams. She often awoke bathed in sweat, screaming and ranting about the moonlight on Montecassino. Her husband Alfonso tried to reason with his heavily pregnant wife and when that no longer helped, even through all the screaming, he tried to calm her down – yet Concetta would not be settled. The fear that this unborn child would bring shame upon the whole family was deeply anchored in her soul.

It was bad enough that the MùMille family had to scrape a bleak existence in their modest fisherman's house in Resina, a small village at the foot of Mount Vesuvius. In 1921 the catch was not what it once was and Alfonso earned hardly enough to feed the eight mouths in his family. Every additional child would bring this large family ever closer to the limits of the unendurable.

Excavations were still going on there – just twenty metres beneath the centre of the village they had started to systematically hollow out all of Resina.

Allegedly, beneath the ten metre thick layer of lava ash, was the splendid city of Herculaneum, which had been razed to the ground in 79 A.D. by the devastating eruption of Mount Vesuvius.

Yet why on earth did Concetta have an interest in the ancient Greeks and in Herculaneum? Papyrus rolls by a certain Epicurus had been salvaged from the Villa dei Papiri – they could just go up in flames, to hell with these damned excavators and the whole pack of archaeologists! Not under any circumstances did she want her house to be hollowed out, or relinquished, no matter what treasures they might find under it; never! And to add to all the irritations and constant summer heat there was now this seventh child, with its weak constitution. At first Concetta thought that Tinor could not absorb the milk from his wet-nurse. Each time he lay there in his little bed, pale, when his sullen wet-nurse had brought him back. Even after he stopped breastfeeding the little boy was often poorly. Bouts of fever alternated with fits of shivering; sometimes the child had diarrhoea, shortly afterwards he vomited. At times he refused his food, at others he was beset with a ravenous hunger. On the days which followed his symptoms seemed to suddenly have blown away. In the course of time this made Concetta believe that Tinor was not really ill at all. She had the feeling that he was bringing on these symptoms himself, just to make her life difficult, to pay her back, since she was unable to show or give him the affection which she bestowed upon her girls.

On some days Tinor was so poorly that Concetta took fright and after struggling mentally for a quite a while, finally sent for Doctor Campagnolo whenever Tinor was running such a high temperature that he just about threatened to lose consciousness. But this bastard had to pay it all back; all the doctor's fees – at the very least – that might just save her soul!

In spite of his high fee invoices, the senile village doctor had not been capable of getting a healing process going in Tinor. During each visit he scratched the bald area at the back of his head with is right hand, pensively, perhaps to come up with an idea for a new healing solution; he tried out this medicine and that medicinal herb on the boy, yet nothing really seemed to help. "No cure, no cure", he muttered to himself each time, shaking his head in disbelief. With time Campagnolo too became sullen. He firmly believed in the spirit of the foremost medical traditions of the Salerno Medical School. After all, his family had for generations lived in Campania, and it was right there that the knowledge of Hippocratic and Arabian medicine had been handed down to the Benedictine monks at Montecassino who were able to read and write. This divine union of medical heritage between two different cultures must have brought about the defining moment of modern western medicine. In the sixth century St. Benedict even succeeded in bringing a young dead boy back to life on this mountain – and he, Campagnolo, had failed at the febrile convulsions of this strange, red-haired creature! Why was this brat completely unaffected by every therapeutic approach? It couldn't of course be down to him, after all he was a gifted physician, with a long tradition of healing behind him. The devil must have had his finger in the pie when this child was conceived!

Chapter 2

"Only the person who belongs with the weak themselves, has a sense for the weak. When a doctor carries no weakness in himself, he will not be in a position to help anyone."
Werner Leibbrand

Tinor grew up in his own little world. What else could he do? It was obvious that no-one wanted to have anything to do with him. His parents even tried to keep him away from his own sisters. Even three year-old Lucia, who, after a stillborn child, came into the world two years after Tinor. Lucia was the only one who genuinely took Tinor to her heart. She tenderly stroked Tinor's weak body with her little hands, when her big brother became delirious once again; she tenderly kissed his cheeks, reddened from the fever, until Concetta brusquely snatched the little one away from the boy's sick bed, screaming wildly - so great was her fear that one of her girls might be infected with Tinor's strange illness.

It was also his outer appearance which marked Tinor out as a misfit. He was the only child in the village with light skin and a complexion like translucent wax. The myriad of freckles which covered his face and body and his curly red hair lead the people of Resina to suspect that the black-haired, dark-skinned Alfonso might not even be his biological father. There had always been red-heads in Italy since the reign of Emperor Frederick I, and since ships had crossed the seas and the first Africans landed on the coast of Salerno; there had always been

Negroid faces, curly hair and full, Cupid's bow lips, but of course nobody in the village wanted to know about this. Indeed, Alfonso's surname was MùMille, which presumably had its origins in Eritrea – and that dated back many centuries.

When village gossip about Tinor's possible descent came to Alfonso's attention – since it was the most popular gossip at the time, gripping the imaginations of these coastal dwellers and giving rise to all kinds of speculation, he seethed inside. Since he was not able to endure this awful feeling of rage and impotence and didn't know how he would be able to get rid of it in any other way, when such moments arose he began to drink in the little village bar during the day. As soon as he had consumed a fair bit of alcohol, he stumbled home, complaining wildly, and beat Concetta – and Tinor too for good measure. Till such time as Concetta slid to her knees in front of the fisherman and protested her innocence to him that she would never deceive him and had never wasted a single thought on another man! 'Amore mio, credimi, amo solo te'! Alfonso was the only one she loved, above anyone else. After all, she had known and loved him even at the tender age of 14 when she was still a virgin, through and through. He was the only man in her life who had ever touched her. It was in these moments that Alfonso again felt potent, his masculinity was boosted considerably when Concetta kneeled before him on her grazed knees, crying and begging; she wanted him to believe her, in the hope that Alfonso would finally compose himself, and would not take a swipe again. He then told the gaping children to leave the kitchen, except Lucia and Tinor, who were cowering in a corner. He sat down on an old wooden chair and hastily opened his fly. With his right hand he grabbed hold of Concetta's long black hair brusquely, pulled her to him and, beside himself with rage, yelled, 'You are all sluts! The whole house is full of whores! And you have brought a brat to my home and I now have to support it! You miserable liar, you deceived me but now I'll show you that you should never betray Alfonso!"

Concetta was forced to stuff his penis into her mouth, until she retched and could no longer breathe. But Alfonso didn't care; he was the man of the house and she was the mother of a bastard – something she had to atone for, time and again. When Alfonso finally came, he shouted out and said to Lucia, who was hiding in the corner whimpering with fear, embracing Tinor tightly – 'Do you see; this is what happens when you are a slag. Remember that and don't screw about, or you're next!"

Then he kicked Concetta away roughly with his foot. With a satisfied grunt Alfonso zipped up his fly and went to bed. In the evening he went down to the coast and set to sea with the other fishermen as if nothing had happened. Yes, now and then you have to take care of things at home, he said casually to the other fishermen. Without a firm hand in these hard times, it's hard to manage a large family, someone has to take care of orderliness. The other men nodded in silence.On days like this Concetta wished desperately that she were not the mother of this red-haired creature. During her pregnancy she had anticipated how it would all pan out – but the reality was much worse than her night-time visions. Why had God punished her in this way? Why had he made her family the scorn of all of Naples? Why had God placed a bastardo like this in her home? I cannot trust men, thought Concetta, they are cold and unpredictable.

And God is a man too.

Chapter 3

*"He is not a doctor who is not aware of what is
invisible, that which has no name, which has no subject
matter and yet which is effective."*
Paracelsus

In the times when he was not in an illness phase Tinor
crept, quietly tip-toeing and as swiftly as he was able, out
of the house before the sun had risen. The further he got
away from Resina, the better he felt. In the hot summer
months the morning hours were especially precious to
him, when the sun had just risen on the horizon and the
natural surroundings awoke with new life with these first
tender rays, and the full heat of midday had not yet burst
forth over Southern Italy. All alone, the child strolled
around the area; it almost seemed as if Tinor had found in
nature a replacement for affection, which people were not
able to give him.

On his long walks the boy had come up with a game –
when he saw a new little plant, he paused respectfully in
front of it, examined it lovingly, spoke to it and tried to
empathise fully with the plant, to become totally at one
with its unique presence. The large number of species
which thrived on the fertile lava soil in the Gulf of
Naples, was more diverse than anywhere else in Italy and
the child discovered new wonders of the kingdom of
nature on every walk; his game was never ending. Tinor
walked in the forest, in the aromatic lemon and orange
groves and around the vineyards, pinched wonderfully
aromatic San Marzano tomatoes, spoke to the colourful
birds, and in the evening wholly devoted himself to the

tranquillity, depth and the endless expanse of the azure blue sea. When Tinor went on walks at the coast, it was the view to the rocky, rugged Sorrento Peninsula which he loved the most, and to the flower island of Capri, sitting proudly enthroned in the sea, which had been celebrated by many poets since the beginning of time as the embodiment of beauty.

In the twilight of the setting sun, Capri looked like a splendid temple jutting out of the sea, surrounded by brightly glistening diamonds. Tinor was deeply drawn by the charm and magic of this view, the scent and the divine beauty of this paradisiacal landscape. When he was ill again and had to stay in bed, he thought about Capri and the sparkling gemstones, about which he would tell stories when he was delirious with fever. He imagined he was sitting at the sea, listening to the soft whispering of the waves, which told him of hope and love and gently stroked his soul. On occasions when his fever was so great, he became a seagull. He left his fever-weary body, soared high into the blue skies, wings outstretched, and glided with ease and grace above the sea, as though he had never had a heavy body which kept him on the ground and inflicted pain upon him.

So it was that Tinor sank wholly into his own inner realm, into his own little paradise, to be able to endure the life which was unfolding around him. He even liked being confined to bed; his spirit was free as the breezy flight of the seagull. His father could rant and rave at him as much as he liked, it had no bearing on his tender soul. It was almost as if a bank of fog opened up in front of his little paradise during every squabble, which on the one hand the external attacks bounced off and on the other, provided protection and watched over his paradise, so his sensitive little soul was able to survive within it. This bank of fog also helped when Doctor Campagnolo poured Tinor another new bitter herbal drink – the child simply gulped it down since he had long ago given up trying to resist. Tinor simply did what others asked of him, without protest, since he had quickly learned that the less resistance he offered, the less of a target he provided. He was acting, in and a way, and was indeed there in body, but in spirit he was in his beloved natural surroundings.

When on his long walks Tinor observed the beauty of the mountains and the bizarre cliffs and took a deep breath, taking in the scents of Bougainvillea, azaleas and orange blossoms, fixing them firmly in his consciousness, it was impossible for his sentient soul to understand quite why there was bickering and hatred in his, or in any other family. There was actually nothing more to do than to open your heart and thank God for this paradise on earth.

Tinor had no more burning desire than to finally recover, so that one day after an excursion he might no longer have to head back to Resina to this house. He wanted – his childlike imagination was indeed brimming with vividness – to live far away from everybody. Maybe on a little island like Capri, in a simple, modest hut by the sea. He would plant flowers and herbs and watch them grow, far away from the clamour of people; in tranquillity.

However he did want to go to the big city too, to Naples. As soon as he was finally better he would look for the cathedral there, to pray to San Gennaro, the patron saint of the city. The former Bishop of Benevento was decapitated in 304 A.D. A woman collected the blood of the martyr in a vial – so the legend about the saint went and Tinor had heard this time and again in the little church in Resina. She had never let go of it – the dried blood of the Patron Saint of Naples had been kept in the cathedral for almost 600 years, and every year since then it was liquidified on three memorial days, when, in a celebratory, ecstatic ceremony, the archbishop brought the vial of blood close to the remains of the saint, who had been laid to rest in the catacombs of the cathedral. Tinor absolutely wanted to see this miraculous blood from Naples once, since it augured that no misfortune would occur in the future.

Chapter 4

"Like cures like! – This is a command, an imperative, the beginning of the Acts of the Apostles."
Herbert Fritsche

By the age of five Tinor had also discovered his passion for archaeological excavations. But what interested him much more than Herculaneum beneath his home village of Resina, were the excavations in Pompeii further east. Thanks to the archaeologist Amedeo Maiuri, who had taken on the scientific supervision there in 1924, the excavations there were already much more advanced in Pompeii than they were in Herculaneum.

As often as Tinor's delicate state of health enabled him, the little boy crept out of the house early in the morning and set out on an hour's walk from Resina in the heart of the country, to the foot of Mount Vesuvius.

Just before the excavation sites his route took him through the Valle di Pompeii, an emergent Christian pilgrimage destination, whose famous landmark was the Santuario della Madonna del Rosario church. Tinor had a little break each time and went into the cool pilgrimage church. For the most part he was the only visitor in the morning. A few hours later numerous pilgrims from all over the world would walk up the steps to the church, to then prostrate themselves in front of the entrance portal, kiss the holy ground and finally gather around the picture of Our Lady of the Rosary above the altar; the church of the Blessed Mother in Pompeii had become the most visited pilgrimage church in Italy after Rome, and even Assisi. Tinor reverently entered the church and breathed in the air, cold and heavy with frankincense. He went to the altar and knelt in front of the impressive painting of the Mother of God. He then clasped his hands and in silent prayer appealed profoundly to the Blessed Virgin that she might heal him of this terrible illness. Since he believed that old Doctor Campagnolo and his bitter medicinal drinks could not help him. Where else could he find a remedy, other than with her?

He looked upon the picture of the Mother of God for a long time and each time it seemed to him that she was smiling kindly at him. Tinor then felt a gentle wisp of wind, woven from the fabric of mercy, and it made his body shudder. The child stood up from the altar with a new vigour, crossed himself and continued on his way to the nearby excavation sites of ancient Pompeii.

In the ruins of old Pompeii the young boy was able to let his imagination run free, helping him forget about the dramas, which were almost a daily occurrence, for a short time at least. When Tinor jumped around in the ruins and piles of stones, he was plunged into a completely new realm. Vivid images appeared before his mind's eye; how vibrant Roman life would have looked before Vesuvius' major eruption. He saw thriving businesses in the most lucent colours, spas, the Temple of Isis, the amphitheatre, the splendid houses which had slaves' quarters and the quadratic design of the internal gardens. Healing plants, which would have been grown in these gardens along with fruit and vegetables, also emerged before his mind's eye.

When Tinor then met the archaeologist Maiuri, he always asked him about these plants, what exactly would have been there and in particular, what illnesses they aided. The archaeologist knew absolutely nothing about botanical medicine, which interested him very little, yet nonetheless his eyes sparkled when he then told Tinor about the legendary discovery of Gaius Plinius Secundus, Pliny the Elder. The former commander of the imperial fleet, historian and natural scientist, had left behind an almost completely preserved 37-volume work, 'Naturalis historica', presumed to be the oldest surviving encyclopaedia of natural history. Pliny, when he heard about the eruption of Vesuvius, travelled to Stabiae, a village close to Pompeii to help friends. It was there that he too perished, from the fumes of the volcano. Unfortunately he did not have the sense to show Tinor the 'Naturalis historica', after all he probably could not read or write, nor presumably would he ever learn to.

Frustrated, Tinor then left. Had he been able to read and write, then he may perhaps have been able to study such works about plants himself and maybe even come across a rare healing plant which would have been able to alleviate his illness. But Maiuri was probably right. There was no sense in showing Tinor the encyclopaedia.

Nonetheless the architect always liked talking to this strange looking boy who came, barefoot, to see him every few weeks. Something about this emaciated boy fascinated Maiuri, who, like him, also enthusiastically spent every available minute in the heat of the midday sun in the rubble, and he always surprised him with his bright intellect and the most peculiar questions – questions that you would never expect from a five year-old. Other children who occasionally hung around the excavations and to some extent even impeded them considerably, only wanted to know something about the battles of the ancient Romans, or how dreadful it must have been in 79 A.D. when Vesuvius started to erupt, spewing fire over the Gulf of Naples, and when the ferocious north wind had driven a thick layer of smoke and ash across the flourishing town of Pompeii, immediately burying all life beneath it – and this pale, red-haired lad was only interested in plants. That was hard to grasp!

On occasions when the pitiful appearance of this little one aroused pity in the archaeologist, he even slipped him a few coins so he could buy himself something better to wear, or at least at some point a pair of shoes. Tinor then bought something for Lucia.

When Concetta then saw Lucia's new shoes, she shouted at Tinor:

"You little thief, where did you pinch the money to buy brand-new shoes for your little sister? Or did you steal them from the old shoe shop in Valle die Pompeii? I knew it!", screamed Concetta beside herself with rage, "you will only bring shame to our family! You good-for-nothing, you hang about somewhere all day long and leave your father and I all alone here to slave away!"

But she soon quietened down again – at least her little glimmer of light, Lucia, had shoes – and that was the most important thing!

Chapter 5

"For a person who seems to be beset by incompatibility, only love succeeds. Altruism is literally "the method of choice" in coming up with homeopathic medicines."
Herbert Fritsche

A fortnight passed where Tinor again had to stay in bed, febrile convulsions sapped his weak little body, which weighed just 20 kilos. Doctor Campagnolo did his best and again poured the child all sorts of bitters, expensive medicines, but no medication seemed to have even remotely an effect on Tinor.

In this terrible illness phase Tinor learned about the death of Bartolo Longo. It was 1926, and news spread around all of Italy like wildfire. Tinor had never known the at that time famous religious man in person, but he knew of his kindness and compassion, after all it was Bartolo Longo, who had in 1875 had built Tinor's favourite church, the Santuario della Madonna del Rosario in Valle di Pompeii. The eminent jurist, who evidently loved the ruins of Pompeii very much and frequently went walking there, had had a mysterious experience in the gardens of Pompeii one evening, about which he reported the following:

"On this evening I was very confused and had been contemplating suicide when I suddenly heard an echo in my ear, which repeated the words of the Blessed Virgin:

If you are in search of healing, then say the rosary, this is Maria's promise.

These words lit up my soul and I fell to my knees and said to myself, if this is true then I will never leave this valley and will proclaim Maria's message of salvation".

After this mysterious experience, Bartolo Longo asked the inhabitants of the area to help him build a church. Since he has no money to have an expensive, beautiful picture of the Virgin Mary made, he accepted a gift from a nun in Porta Medina, an ancient picture of the Virgin Mary, which was brought to Valle di Pompeii from the harbour town close to Naples in a wagon so it could be restored there.

On the first evening after the completion of the future pilgrimage church only a few children came to say the rosary with Bartolo Longo. Somewhat later a few adults also joined, and within the next few months the first Marian apparitions and miracle healings occurred. 20 years later hundreds of miracles then occurred and the Vatican officially recognised the Basilica of the Blessed Mother of the Holy Rosary as a pilgrimage church. Pope Leo XIII even became an emissary of the miracle which occurred in Pompeii and called to pilgrims throughout the world:

"Go to Pompeii and pray for the Pope in the Pontiff's pilgrimage church!"

Bartolo Longo's death was a heavy blow to Tinor, he had even hoped many times to be able to catch sight of the religious man at least once, somewhere in Valle di Pompeii. But that would now no longer be possible.

Years after Bartolo Longo's death an inscription beneath the picture of the Queen of the Rosary seemed to say to pilgrims from all over the world what Tinor had also felt inside, each time he visited the church:

"In front of this image the soul in prayer feels the firm hope that it is being heard and that ineffable sweetness which is only comprehensible to those to whom this is conferred".

Tinor felt magically drawn to this picture of the Virgin Mother. When he seemed to have recovered from his fever somewhat, he immediately made his way back to the pilgrimage church, to pray a rosary in loving memory of the departed Bartolo Longo. This time he took the shortest route, not through the fragrant orange groves, but on the parched roads which ran from Resina directly to Pompeii.

The child traipsed barefoot in the heat of the midday sun. He had to stop from time to time since he broke into a sweat and his whole body trembled. Weak and covered in scratches from the stony road, Tinor finally reached the entrance portal of the church, where he had to rest first of all. Wheezing, he sat down on the stone steps at the portal of the church and using his shirt, which clung to his sweaty body, tried to wipe the sweat from his face which had gone into his eyes, which were burning terribly.

In his exhaustion, Tinor did not at first notice that someone was approaching him in the distance. Due to his poor sight he saw only a shadowy form at first, which looked like it was enshrouded in a silver mist, and was moving slowly towards him.

"Holy Virgin Mary, this is the end", thought the young boy, "this is what it must feel like when you are dying."

The image then slowly became more clear, the mist cleared somewhat and the young boy screwed up his eyes to be able to see better against the light of the sun. He now caught sight of a heavy-set, cheerful looking man in a long, dark-brown habit and leather sandals. The habit, which was laced tightly with cord, at once accentuated the monk's corpulence. The stranger sat down stolidly beside Tinor on the steps, scrutinised him with an affectionate look and then asked him where he came from, whether he were ill and if he went to school. Tinor answered politely that he was the only son of Concetta and Alfonso from Resina, that he was well but that he would probably never go to school since his parents, the MùMilles, did not have very much money and that he was also probably too stupid for school. His parents had told him that time and again. The Father immediately recognised the poor mental and physical constitution of the boy and responded:

"I am Monsignore Umberto Ronca from Rome, and am successor here in Pompeii to the blessed Bartolo Longo, who spread the message of Mary and spent his life in the orphanages, which he had built himself, to see to children's education. The well-being of all children is something which is also dear to my heart and as long as I see but one unhappy child, I will not rest and my soul will not find peace – in three days I will look for your parents in Resina."

Ronca's reason to see to the well-being of such a shabby ragamuffin, may perhaps have arisen from his magnanimity and charity. Yet maybe too it was that initial enthusiasm which everyone feels whey they take on a new post or a new task. No obstacle seems to be too great in this event; even the impossible can be ventured. Ronca blessed the young boy, as he made the sign of the cross on his forehead, stroke his red, curly hair, wet with sweat and then disappeared as silently and as quickly and unexpectedly as he had arrived, in the portal of the church.

Confused by this brief encounter and by the words of the reverend Monsignore, Tinor continued to sit for a while on the steps in front of the impressive church portal. When he stood up and wanted to go into the church, he became dizzy again. Yet with every last ounce of strength, he dragged himself up to the picture of the Virgin Mary, bent down and prayed a rosary to the memory of Bartolo Longo and then decided to return home again. He felt too weak to spend the day at the excavation site with Maiuri.

Throughout his journey home, Tinor thought about his discussion with the Monsignore. But the closer he got to his home village, the more surreal this meeting seemed to him. When Tinor entered the house, his mother rushed up to him and screamed:

"The doctor said that you were to stay in bed, what are you doing running around? Look at you; pale as death, dark circles under your eyes and bathed in sweat! It's no wonder you never get healthy, when you run about with a fever. Now get out of my sight, you good-for-nothing!"

"Mama", began Tinor with a weak, soft voice, "Mama, the Monsignore is coming to visit you in a few days".

"Who is this Monsignore?"

"He's the new Monsignore from Pompeii".

"Monsignore Ronca?", screamed Concetta hysterically, her voice almost cracking, "you are a fantasist! What would Ronca be doing in Resina?

He goes to the Pope in Rome, he won't come to me! I think you're now delusional, you blasphemer; what am I to do with you?"

Concetta sat herself down at the kitchen table in despair, held her head in her hands and sobbed incessantly. "Clear off", muttered one of his big sisters to him and gave him a push, "get to bed, don't you see that you are going to send our mother to her grave in misery!"

Tinor took himself to his bed. He slept and slept and slept. When, between fever attacks, something came to him again, he did not know how much time had passed; was it hours or days? But that did not really have any major role to play in his life. From time to time he thought about the Monsignore. His mother was probably right, and it actually all just been a dream, wishful thinking, which had arisen from a brain overheated with fever.

Chapter 6

"Symptoms reveal not only the illness, but also that which will bring about healing."
Herbert Fritsche

Three days later there was a knock on the MùMille's wooden front door. When Concetta opened the door and saw who was standing in front of her, she gasped briefly and held the doorframe tightly; she thought she was on the verge of fainting. The venerable Monsignore Ronca and his female companion, the somewhat elderly Benedictine nun Giulia Fratelli, asked to be admitted:

"Buon giorno, signora!", said Ronca, short of breath, as he shuffled his ample corpulence through the little door frame of the house and purposefully headed for the kitchen in the centre of the house. It was a moment before Concetta regained her composure and offered the Monsignore and Sister Giulia seats. She too then sat down at the kitchen table with the visitors.

"Signora, we are here because we are concerned about the well-being of your little Tinor", spoke Ronca and after a brief pause, continued, with a concerned expression. "I met him by chance a few days ago in in Valle di Pompeii. The little one was sitting on the steps of the entrance portal of the pilgrimage church and I had the impression that he was very ill. That was why I spoke to him. Please excuse me for intruding upon your private affairs in such a way. It is of course nothing to do with me, but what is it that your son needs? Is he very ill? Is he getting the right medical care and attention?" Concetta was speechless at first, she sat with her mouth half open and didn't know how she should reply. An emissary of the Pope in Rome had come to her humble abode in Resina and was worried about the well-being of this good-for-nothing! As if Ronca had nothing more important to be doing! As if the church did not have any other problems! For pity's sake, this was a little strange. The whole village would have of course have observed that the clergyman and the Sister had come to her house. This visit would provide sufficient topic for conversation in Resina for the next few decades to come. But Concetta soon more or less had herself under control again. She gasped for breath once again, then put on the expression of the suffering mother – which had become all too familiar to her in the last few years – and appealed to the Monsignore and Sister Giulia:

"Since Tinor has been in this world he has been so ill, the poor, poor child! He has suffered from unsettling bouts of fever, but Doctor Campagnolo does not quite know what illness it is. Can no-one help my poor child! We have already spent our last savings on expensive medication. You cannot imagine just how desperate I am! You don't know how awful it is to be a mother who can do nothing to help her sick child...", sobbed Concetta.

"There are of course healers, what I mean is real healing artists, who may be able to help your son, Signora", resumed Ronca in his quiet, resonant voice, "I would like to propose a suggestion, if I may, since I am guessing that you have no other financial means to consult other doctors and specialists. If you agree, I am offering to take Tinor with us. We will accommodate him in one of Bartolo Longo's orphanages. We will see to his medical care and will send your son to school.

I cannot promise that your son will be healed and will be restored to health – I am of course not God! – but it might be worth a visit to another doctor might be worth it in any case, what do you think?"

This was too much for Concetta. She staggered up, turned for a brief moment from the Monsignore and the taciturn Benedictine sister, looked fixedly at the opposite wall in the kitchen and tried to organise the thoughts circulating in her head as quickly as possible. Why should such great benevolence be bestowed upon their little bastard? Why was the Monsignore even bothering himself with him and not he wonderful daughters?

Yet in spite of her resentful thoughts, she was jubilant inside, since at last she was offered a long yearned for opportunity to get rid of Tinor. And in a manner which would make her look good in the eyes of the other villagers. She would tell her neighbour Gilda straight away – a son in the monastery, chosen by the venerable Monsignore Ronca – that counted for a lot in Southern Italy.

When the widow Gilda, who had some difficulty walking, learned of this news, you could be sure that she would soon be scurrying through the alleys of Resina like a weasel. The rumour would then spread throughout the Gulf of Naples as fast as an explosive lava cloud, and a haze of truth and hearsay would drift across every village in a flash! Great, that could only be the right thing to do, pondered Concetta further! Peace and normality would then finally return to her home! Alfonso would then certainly be appeased; he would no longer see the boy and the daily sight of Tinor would not trigger rage within him. It would seem that God had listened to her prayers and cries for help, when he sent to the Monsignore to her! With tears in her eyes Concetta turned to the Monsignore and Sister Giulia:

"Yes, venerable Monsignore, venerable Sister, if you think that is the best thing for my child, then I agree of course, even if it almost breaks my heart that I have to part with one of my dear children. I recognise of course divine grace and the great opportunity for my son, in your kind offer".

"Should we not see what your husband thinks?", asked Ronca, who found the spontaneous decision of a mother to part with her child, really quite disconcerting. Yet at the same time he was also certain that it was good at that time to listen to his inner voice and to help this child. The visit to Resina was the correct decision and Ronca thanked his God inwardly for this prudent guidance.

"Oh no, Monsignore, I know that this decision will also make my husband Alfonso overjoyed. We would never be able to reject your generous offer even though it is with a heavy heart. Our only heart's desire is for our child to become healthy again. We have prayed to God for years for this and done penance. When would you like to take Tinor with you?"

"If you want, right away, should Tinor's condition permit", replied Ronca, "we have already prepared everything in the orphanage for his arrival."

Concetta fell to her knees before the venerable Monsignore, took his warm podgy hands in hers as a gesture of overwhelming gratitude, kissed him fervently and let her tears fall.

She then hurried to Tinor's room to get him, but the boy had already fallen asleep. Concetta roughly shook the child's shoulders, to get him to wake up more quickly. She then lifted up Tinor by one arm so he had to sit up in bed, half-asleep.

"Monsignore Ronca is here and is taking you away. Go with him, that will be the best for all of us. I will pack your things now; get dressed!"

Concetta ran and fetched a shabby bag in which, with a few flicks of the wrist, she stuffed a few of Tinor's tatty clothes. She then thrust the confused little boy in front of her into the kitchen and the Monsignore greeted Tinor, explaining to him in a friendly way what his plans for him were. Without hesitation, Tinor picked up his bag and politely said goodbye to his mother, even though at the moment he did not know what was happening to him.

He was about to go when he suddenly caught sight of little Lucia, who was peering surreptitiously through the kitchen door which was ajar. Tinor put down his bag again, ran to his little sister and threw his arms around her to say his goodbyes. He stroked her tresses from her face and with tears in eyes said to her, lovingly:

"You are my only glimmer of hope little Lucia, I will never forget you. Please don't forget me either."

Then Sister Giulia took Tinor unfalteringly by the hand, and they and the Monsignore left the house together.

Chapter 7

"I now believe more keenly than ever in the doctrines of the wondrous doctor, since I so vigorously felt, and time and again still feel, the effect of the tiniest dose."

Johann Wolfgang v. Goethe in a letter dated 2nd September 1820 about Samuel Hahnemann

Ronca took Tinor straight to the orphanage in Valle di Pompeii, which was close to the pilgrimage church. Sister Giulia accompanied the boy to his new room. It had a clean bed and a cabinet, and from the window you could see right onto the main piazza, in the middle of which the Santuario della Madonna del Rosario sat enthroned.

The gentle Benedictine sister organised fresh linen from the clothing store for Tinor and told him to go to bed. She knew that the little one was too weak to eat his evening meal with the other children in the dining hall that evening, so she brought some soup and a glass of warm milk to his room. She then sat on the edge of his bed, gently caressed the boy's red, curly locks and told him that tomorrow morning a doctor from Naples would come to him to make him better, so he would then soon be able to play with the other children and go to school.

Tinor didn't know what had happened to him. The experience that adults were pleasant to him, was not something which had happened too often in his short life. In fact, it was only once until now; he was thinking in particular about the architect Maiuri.

His parents and Doctor Campagnolo blatantly hated

him and the other people in his local village whispered behind closed doors about him, when they saw him walking around the alleys. In the past playing with other children was Tinor's most heartfelt wish. Romping around the beautiful beaches with the crowds of village children, building giant sand castles and frolicking in the warm sea water – what on this earth could have been nicer than that? Yet he had been bitterly disappointed with his every attempt to join in with the village children, when the others suddenly ganged together into little groups, teasing him and even making up rhymes about him which they yelled together in chorus, for instance, "Tinor, what an awful red mop, you must be from some another plot" and "Watch out for those freckly specks, were they made on the African continent?"

Tinor's tender soul often could not endure this humiliation and so he withdrew and became more and more of a loner. In the end he no longer trusted the other children, he feared they might even beat him if they met him somewhere where there was nobody watching.

Tinor didn't think about this for much longer that evening, his exhaustion was too great and it overwhelmed him; he soon fell into a restless sleep.

It was very late when the child awoke the next morning. The church bells were ringing incessantly and the sun was already casting slender rays through the cracks of the closed window shutters onto the stone floor in the room. Tinor had a fever again and when he was awoken by the loud peal of bells he didn't know at first where he was at all. Everything seemed strange to him, he only saw the rays of light falling into the room and thought that he might have died and the Blessed Virgin had come to take him home.

Suddenly there was a knock at the door and Sister Giulia entered the room with a man, who was carrying a battered, leather doctor's case in his right hand. Sister Giulia opened the shutters first of all and from the heat which poured into the room, it was immediately clear that today too, this heat would set in over all of Campania from early morning. Tinor slowly remembered where he was and how he had got there. The unfamiliar man, who seemed to be very friendly, turned to the just awakened child and bent down to him slightly:

"Ciao, Tinor, I am Doctor Sergio Focali from Naples."

The skilled healer was, at around 35 years old, still quite a young doctor. With almost youthful vigour, he sat at the edge of the young boy's bed and looked at him attentively and candidly. First he examined Tinor's pupils, got the boy to show him his tongue and finger nails and asked him a variety of questions – what time was the fever strongest, what food and drink did Tinor take a notion for, whether he was afraid of thunderstorms and all kinds of other things, which initially seemed very odd to Tinor. Nonetheless he obligingly provided the doctor with information, since he liked him straight away. The doctors' black hair, dark-brown eyes and sincere manner instilled deep trust in him.

Focali wrote Tinor's responses meticulously on a piece of paper. He then opened his leather case, in which, along with pigskin case, there were also a few thick, well-thumbed books. Focali took out two of the books, browsed with interest in one book, then in the other and checked various passages again. Then Focali seemed to nod to himself. He shut the books, put them back into his case, took the pigskin case and opened it up. Tinor gazed in wonder at its contents. There were a vast number of little glass tubes, which had tiny white beads in them. Tinor had never seen anything like it before. The Neapolitan doctor opened the cork stopper of one of the tubes, tapped out five beads into his own hand first of all and then placed them in Tinor's hand, asking him to suck on these beads, since there was a power within them to heal him of his severe illness. Tinor did as he was bid and put the sweet tasting beads in his mouth, even though he now thought the doctor was a bit peculiar. Could a medicine that didn't taste bitter help?

Doctor Focali explained to the child that this was a homeopathic medication, and that homeopathy was very different to standard medicine. When he saw Tinor's big, enquiring eyes, the previously somewhat taciturn doctor continued with his remarks, in a non-stop torrent of words, without even considering whether the child was even able to understand him:

"Do you know what, little one, to my knowledge you are suffering from a very, very rare form of malaria, malaria quartana, an exceptionally stubborn form of malaria which occurs in very rare, isolated incidences in the south of Italy. I spoke with Doctor Campagnolo about you. He has already administered all the standard medications from conventional medicine, which are currently available, but they have not been able to heal you. I am a homeopathic practitioner and have a somewhat different philosophy about the course and development of disease, than the majority of scientists. Did you know that a good medicine must stimulate the body's own powers of self-healing." Focali stood up and looked out of the window with a slightly blissful gaze down to the bustling piazza below. He then turned to Tinor again and continued with his monologue:

"The founder of homeopathy, Samuel Hahnemann, said that an illness would upset the body's vital energies; do you understand? So something has got into a state of disorder which means that the body's powers to heal itself can no longer do so properly. Usually the human body is a real marvel, it fights off and destroys pathogens in its stride. Conventional medicine tries to combat the symptoms of an illness. Homeopathy has a different approach entirely, since it starts with a completely different understanding of illness and health. Our sole goal is to put the body's powers of self-healing back on the right track, gently. So when your powers of self-healing are no longer able to do their job optimally, homeopathy puts the body's order right again. It does so by quite simply using medications which are similar to the ailment. Yes, I know it all sounds a bit crazy, doesn't it?"

Amused, Focali looked at Tinor, who seemed to have several questions written all over his face. After a short pause, the doctor continued with is explanations:

"I have just administered you a homeopathic medication - china-bark - which, if it were administered at full strength to a healthy person, would elicit the exact symptoms which you have in your condition now - recurrent attacks of fever, shivering fits, bouts of sweating and poor circulation of the blood. Of course, in homeopathy these medications are not administered neat – or else they would be highly toxic, like belladonna -

deadly nightshade - which may even cause delirium and death – so a homeopathic medicine is diluted in a water-alcohol mixture, in only the amount that it contains the healing information the body, soul and spirit needs, but none of the components which might be toxic to the body. In homeopathy this is called the process of dilution, or potentiation. It's as simple as that!"

"Focali now looked visibly delighted to have found a good explanation for Tinor, for his objective was always that his patients would understand homeopathy and the healing process associated with it:

"It may be that for you there will be an initial aggravation which might perhaps make the fever stronger, but this is completely normal and you shouldn't fret about it. Quite the opposite, you can then be quite sure that the remedy has started the healing process in you! I will come back in a few days to see you. Until then, get plenty of rest my boy, and don't worry. You are in good hands with Monsignore Ronca."

Focali remained by the boy's sick bed for a moment longer, then added briefly:

"By the way, I knew your mother a few years ago; she was a very pretty young woman. Give her my regards. And if you can't remember my name, then just say: the moonlight on the Montecassino".

The doctor then took his leave of the child, who was by this time completely confused and asked Sister Giulia to ensure that Tinor observed the requisite period bed rest, at least two days.

Chapter 8

"Who doesn't recognise the infinite virtue of the (homeopathic) doctor, using means of similar influence, the pitiful method of opposites (contraria contrariis), in accordance with the ancient and common art of healing?"
Samuel Hahnemann

After about a week the child was almost completely recovered and it seemed that Tinor, in the same way in which his illness abated, had said goodbye to his childhood and had just discarded it like a coat which had become too small.

When he felt completely healthy again, he begged Sister Giulia to allow him to go home for a short time to pray in the Madonna of the Rosary pilgrimage church.

"But Tinor, you can still pray in the little orphanage chapel", suggested the Sister kindly. If you go from the main building of the orphanage through a path lined by stone columns, pines and Bougainvilla to the cloister garden, at the other end of the parks you can get directly to the chapel. It is open to the pupils at any time for prayer for inner contemplation.

Tinor did not respond to Sister Giulia's suggestion, he just gave her a beseeching look with his big brown eyes. She had taken this misfit to heart and knew that Tinor had a good character and that for his age that he was an exceptionally sensible child, who didn't make a fuss about anything, or run away from anything. So she finally allowed him to go and pray for half an hour in the Santuario della Madonna del Rosario.

Upon arrival at the pilgrimage church, Tinor once again knelt at the altar in front of the picture of the Virgin Mary and thanked the Mother of God for hearing his prayers and for the miracle of his cure. Tinor then said a rosary for Doctor Focali and gave Mary his word of honour that he too would become a homeopathic practitioner, as long as he were not too stupid for school, so he could help other people and liberate them from their suffering – even though at this juncture he neither knew exactly what a homeopathic practitioner was, nor, how he could become one. For he hadn't actually really understood what Focali had had been trying to explain to him on his sick bed. Or maybe because of the fever he was not able to remember properly. But at this sacred moment he was also completely unconcerned. At this very second, Tinor knew only one thing for sure – he wanted to become a homoeopathist.

At the age of seven Tinor was sent to school. Even his parents and sisters came to Valle di Pompeii for this celebratory occasion, all of whom he had not seen for almost a year, even though the orphanage was only an hour's walk from Resina. It seemed that they had not missed one another. Tinor's parents and his six older sisters greeted him as formally as though they were standing in front of a stranger who had scabies. Only with Lucia was it different. Her dark child-like eyes beamed when she saw her big brother and then embraced him tightly in her little arms.

In the dining hall in the orphanage a celebratory meal was taken with all the children who were starting school, along with their relatives – if they had any –, there were also the patrons of the orphanage, the teachers and of course Monsignore Ronca, who made an impressive speech for this joyous occasion.

During the meal Alfonso stared vacantly at this plate; not once did he lift his gaze. He poked his pasta about as though he were simple. It also looked like Concetta did not feel good in her skin during this visit. Initially she was derided in the village as the mother of a little bastard, now people spoke ill of her; that she was an uncaring mother who had just shunted off her son to a home. You can never please everyone! But she always preferred the mean gossip, than to have this misfit in her home. If it weren't for this celebration for the first day of his schooling, she would presumably not have visited Tinor. She also considered Tinor's school visit to be wholly unnecessary; what was the point of sending such a simpleton to school? After all, she herself had only gone to school for three years and she certainly made something of herself

"Ok", she thought to herself, "if the honourable Monsignore has so decided that he should send Tinor to school, he will soon see what it is he is dealing with" – the main thing for her was that she didn't have to pay any school fees!

Tinor wasn't particularly in the mood for his first day at school either. After all up to now he only knew that he was a dunce, and he was very afraid that this would be confirmed in school. In spite of this, he definitely wanted to be a good pupil, since he felt that he owed this to the Monsignore and to Sister Giulia for their compassion, because he wanted to become a homoeopathist and because he wanted to prove to his parents and sisters, and all of Resina that he was not a good-for-nothing; that they had just been wrong about him and something might indeed become of him!

In actual fact Tinor struggled with this inner pressure a great deal in the first few weeks of school. He continually suffered headaches, often felt pressure in his ears and was not able to follow a lesson properly. When a teacher asked him something, for the most part he did know the answer, but before he could even say anything, he was overcome by a sort of anxiety. It was almost as if a black cloud of oblivion descended upon his conscience for a moment, with the result that he no longer knew and could not even remember the teacher's question. His classmates laughed each time and slapped their thighs when Tinor could not provide an answer to the simplest of questions. The boy was accustomed to the feeling of being a wretched failure from his earliest childhood days and so took this humiliation relatively calmly.

Maybe it was this new composure which gradually helped him become calmer. For after a few weeks of settling in, everything suddenly changed. It was as if a completely new world suddenly opened up in front of Tinor – the world of the spirit. To him, it seemed as if a curtain had been raised. Before everything had been dark, now suddenly everything was light and bright. To the young boy it felt as though the sun was now shining right into his brain, illuminating the subject matter so he was able to see and understand it. Eager to learn, he from then on he absorbed everything that his teachers imparted to him. His classmates' laughter swiftly fell silent and it was only a few months before Tinor was the exemplary pupil of the entire orphanage school. Monsignore Ronca's joy was naturally enormous, since it had been he who had brought this boy prodigy to his orphanage, almost directly from the gutter.

Tinor also had only little contact with the other children in the home, also because he quickly intellectually outgrew the pupils of the same-age in his class. He also devoted his free time solely to learning. Even after his first year at school, Tinor's teachers began to eagerly persuade the Monsignore, that Tinor must possess an exceptional intelligence quotient, something about which they were agreed upon. They had never experienced such a child in all of their teaching careers and Tinor had to be nurtured, since he was completely unchallenged in the local village school in Valle di Pompeii. Monsignore Ronca of course felt exceptionally flattered by the teachers. That he had done such a stellar turn for this peculiar looking child, was something he attributed to divine guidance, which he believed had been bestowed upon him the first time he met Tinor.

After a while Ronca finally agreed that Tinor should be sent to a better school in Naples. Indeed that would certainly cost a small fortune, but people in Rome would also learn that he, Monsignore Ronca, was such an exceptional patron and a promoter of good scholastic education. The Pope would certainly hear about the boy prodigy and it was through this that the doors to a career in the Vatican might open for Ronca.

Chapter 9

"The homeopathic principles, once known, are plain, simple and easily understandable. They are in harmony with all things known to be true."
James Tyler Kent

Just a few weeks after Tinor's transfer to the secondary school in the historic city of Naples, it became clear that this educational establishment was also not nearly able to do justice to his intellectual capacities. It was therefore agreed in the staff meeting that the boy should jump two classes, since too few demands were placed upon his intellectual abilities. In the afternoon he was also permitted to participate in optional subjects, which were otherwise only taken by pupils who were a few years older than him. At the age of eleven, Tinor spoke Latin fluently and to the amazement of all his teachers translated, with the deft ease of a native speaker, Caesar's "de bello gallico", a classic which other pupils were still only able to rather poorly translate, even after several years of studying Latin.

Tinor's parents and sisters had not visited him since that celebratory first day of school, even though news had of course also permeated to Resina of this highly gifted boy prodigy – the ginger genius, as the envious scornfully called him. Even though from the time of his birth Tinor had not been as loved as his sisters, his parents in their aloofness, were indeed a little bit proud of his scholastic achievements. Concetta was now basking in the glory of being the mother of an über-talented child prodigy, intimating to the other village inhabitants that she had always known that Tinor was something quite special.

It had been an almighty effort for Tinor's sisters to overcome the hurdle of being illiterate, whereas in Tinor, at the age of 14, it was believed that a mathematical genius had been discovered.

Time and again the highly gifted boy was lucky to come across teachers and mentors who recognised and promoted his genius, since they reckoned that a little Einstein was standing before them. After all, it was only a few years previous that Einstein, in the year of Tinor's birth, 1921, had received the Nobel Prize in Physics. Later on they would certainly be able to boast about Tinor's scientific discoveries themselves. Monsignore Ronca too was filled with pride when he received a letter from Rome, in which Giorgio Alberti, private secretary to the Pope, wanted to know what was this unbelievable news about this boy prodigy from the gutter was all about. Ronca replied immediately of course, since he was aware that Alberti was the person who spoke with the Pope most often:

Venerable Monsignore Alberti,

as soon as I saw the young boy sitting on the steps of the church, I heard an inner voice say to me that this child was something quite special. God himself placed him in my care and as a servient shepherd, I was only doing my duty to be a worthy subject to our Lord. And God's reward is now fulfilled, since he has now bestowed upon us faithful Catholics this über-talented boy, who will someday enrich the Catholic Church with his knowledge. Tinor MùMille has just turned 16 years old and has learned seven languages at an incredible speed, among them Latin, Ancient Greek, Hebrew and even Aramaic. What an ineffable treasure he would be for our church, if we think of the translation of the ancient scriptures alone. Even that was not enough - Tinor MùMille has now received special permission to attend the University of Naples and will therefore be the youngest Italian ever to have attended a university.

We are not yet sure which faculty Tinor will choose. Indeed, this choice must be very difficult for him, since his talents lie in language and in natural sciences in equal measure. But we are certain that he will soon make the right choice and someday help the church, and even all of Italy, gain worldwide fame.

Venerable Father, it would be a blessing to me if you could also pass this message to the Pope; he might even possibly want to get to know Italy's youngest genius? Tinor would certainly be aware of the beatific blessing, which has been bestowed upon him, and his decision to enter into his ecclesiastical career as a chaplain, might be affected by him alone.

Yours respectfully,

Monsignore Umberto Ronca

Tinor did not actually understand why so much fuss had been made about him. Learning was no effort at all to him. For him it was more like a re-discovery of long-established knowledge that he merely had to recall. He had the feeling that his conscious mind was like a giant dome, in which all the information had already been compiled. So, neither natural science nor languages presented a real challenge to him.

For the very first time Tinor's life had come to a point where he was expected to make a decision himself - what branch of university studies did he want to choose? Physics, law or humanities? Until now it had always been other people who had made decisions about his life and his academic career, above his head. Yet the matter of what it was he actually wanted to study was something which no-one had asked him.

At first Tinor had wanted to ignore this question, but it always pushed itself into his consciousness. Like an annoying fly that you can't get rid of, even if you swipe at it so many times. It was after all his goal to become a homoeopathist and he sensed that this would deviate from the path, if he now followed the advice of his teachers and mentors. Yet should he resist everything that he achieved, and which he had them to thank for? Ought he to disappoint them?

A great deal of anxiety now arose within Tinor. Sleepless and bathed in sweat, he rolled around in bed at night and considered whether he was actually capable of steering the right course for his own life. Maybe the others actually knew better what was good for him?

Yet increasingly Tinor found that he was more interested in the immaterial, in the ethereal, for that which was unreachable beyond Physics and Astronomy – for pure information. And this was also the reason why Tinor actually did not want to study – if only he had been asked.

Now it seemed that Tinor would for the first time disappoint his mentors, who had firmly believed in him for years, since during a discussion in Ronca's study Tinor very carefully touched upon the fact that he actually did not want to become either a mathematician, a physician like Einstein, nor a theologian, and that he also did not want to study any other sciences worthy of the Nobel Prize.

Ronca gasped for breath initially and blood rushed to his head. He then grasped his heart with his right hand as though it might stop at any moment. He had planned on everything, just not on this.

"Why do you not want to study, Tinor, your entire education – it cannot be for nothing! You shouldn't just simply through a talent like yours away!", said Ronca angrily, gasping for breath. After a brief pause for air he continued:

"Your path has been set out for you! God has gifted you with these unique aptitudes and talents, and if you don't use them, it's as if you are committing a sin!"

The gawky youth stood, embarrassed, with his head hanging, in front of Ronca's huge desk. He now no longer had the courage to say any more. Ronca had given him the feeling that he was a monstrosity of ignorance, and thus it was that Tinor's gaze no longer moved from the old stone floor. Ronca was now snorting, he heaved his body out of the armchair and, on edge, walked up and down his study. He then drew a deep breath, so that his corpulent body almost threated to burst, and continued in a forceful tone:

"Listen Tinor. I took you out of the gutter. I gave you a lovely room, sent a doctor to you, provided you with and paid for the best possible school education. And now you just want to back out? All of Rome is watching both of us! Everyone is waiting intently to see what will become of you now and you, you just want to do nothing? Don't do this to me!"

Ronca shook his head in disbelief. In his mind's eye he had even seen himself as the Pope's closest confidante! Or at the very least a spiritual advisor of a Nobel Prize winner, who might even revolutionise the world with his ideas. Maybe even Ronca's own fame would go so far that he himself might even one day be in the running to become Pope! But what would happen now? Did Tinor actually want to end up as an ice-cream seller in Naples? Or as a fisherman in Sorrento like his father Alfonso? Would Tinor return to the gutter again, from where he had come? Would he just throw away all his talents?

Even Sister Giulia talked insistently and vigorously to Tinor at every opportunity:

"If you really don't want to study, then at least pursue a career in the church! Someone who speaks ancient Greek as fluently as you will be welcomed with open arms by the Vatican!"

These many discussions always ended in the same way - Tinor stood there stoically and no longer replied to the appealing suggestions. After around a fortnight he finally reluctantly enrolled to study medicine. He felt too obliged to the Monsignore, to Sister Giulia, who had almost become a surrogate mother to him, and to all of his teachers and patrons. They had all put such intense efforts into his scholastic career that Tinor saw no other way out than to begin his studies out of gratitude. Except for Maiuri, Focali and his little sister Lucia, they were the only people who had ever looked after his well-being. Even if some of them might have been concealing their own selfish reasons behind a mantle of goodwill.

Chapter 10

"The pure homeopathic healing art, the one possible to human art; is the only correct method, the straightest way to cure as certain as there is but one straight line between two given points."
Samuel Hahnemann

Tinor's patrons and sponsors were on the one hand overjoyed that their pupil had, after a lengthy struggle, now decided to study. Their dream that Tinor would pursue a career in humanities was burst for the time being with his choice to study medicine. And their indignation at this was so great when they learned that Tinor was thinking of studying at the University of Frederick II in Naples. The university's poor reputation in church circles, founded in 1224 by the Germano-Roman Emperor and King of Sicily, Frederick II, was what preceded it. Frederick II opposed the will of the popes at the time and introduced enlightened scientific teaching in the university. The University of Naples thus became one of the only educational establishments in Europe which taught without an official papal seal – something which had always been a thorn in the side of Monsignore Umberto Ronca and the other ecclesiastical dignitaries. Too much free spirit could truly not be good in the long term.

In contrast, Tinor was obviously delighted with the first decision in his life that he had made by himself. He felt the free spirit of this university blow in all its walkways, and the feeling of narrowness which he had often felt under ecclesiastical administration and behind the thick monastery walls in the orphanage, fell away from him like a shadow which had always accompanied him. Tinor felt that it was a good decision that he had accepted the scholarship at the University of Naples, even though he did not know what he would actually do after his studies. But that would become apparent in due course.

Even moving out of the orphanage into a hall of residence at Corso Umberto I had done him good. For the first time in his life Tinor was able to do what he wanted and he indulged in his own private studies every evening.

Just as in previous years Tinor was labelled as a misfit by the other students. He remained the ginger genius from Naples; people coveted his talents and aptitudes, and his withdrawn manner made him seem strange to the majority of people. Yet Tinor was able to deal with the ill humour of the other students in an ever more serene manner; and now that he had his own little student digs for his inner retreat, it was even easier for him than before. Being alone was not a problem for him; it was people who made his life difficult.

Tinor finished his medical studies within four years at University Frederick II in Naples with a summa cum laude, the highest distinction.

It was not only in the Gulf of Naples, all of Italy now celebrated this child prodigy who had now received a doctorate at the age of 20. There was even a big photo of Tinor and Monsignore Ronca on the front page of Naple's biggest newspaper, with the lead article beneath it, "Italy's youngest doctor!" The photograph showed the corpulent Ronca, his chest puffed out with pride, who jovially had his arm around a scraggy young man. He presumably weighed just 50 kilograms and his pale countenance attested to the fact that he did not actually know what was happening to him and what all this razzamatazz was actually about. The author of the lead article was quite certain about Tinor's further career - the brilliant graduation at the medical faculty in Naples should now open up doors around the world for Tinor, to every operating theatre and every research institute. It was probable that there would be loads of offers from all over the world for this young doctor with the golden hands! Tinor would certainly revolutionise modern surgery and come up with new surgical techniques and set milestones in medical history as a pioneering biologist. Who now were Louis Pasteur and Robert Koch in comparison to Italy's youngest medical talent?

Even Giorgio Alberti, private secretary to the Pope, went into raptures in a written congratulation, and in the historic town of Naples many citizens raised the Italian flag on their balconies as a sign of the recognition of Tinor's contributions to his homeland.

On this warm spring evening lots of people gathered exultant and marvelling, in front of the town hall on Piazza del Municipio, as the acting mayor ceremoniously gave Tinor the freedom of Naples. When Tinor received the certificate in front of the town hall and looked bashfully at the crowds of people and thought he caught sight of his mother and a young lady next to her in the back rows. But it surely was not her. He had had no contact with is family for such a long time. He thought wistfully about Lucia, in whose childhood he had been able to play no part. What would she look like today?

Maybe she was indeed the pretty young lady with the brown locks he had just seen.

Of course everybody wanted to know more about this ginger genius on this summer evening, to see him up close or to get an interview for a newspaper. Anyone who wanted to ask him a question, even tugged on his shirt sleeves. But all this commotion and the jostling and murmuring of people was too much for Tinor; he would have preferred to make himself invisible. He quickly stowed away his certificate for the freeman of the city in his bag and hastily left the crowded piazza.

Monsignore Ronca and Tinor's professors and mentors now excitedly awaited his decision as to which university clinic he was now thinking about operating at, and where he would pursue his research; in particular, upon which city he might help bring international renown with his mere presence.

Everyone attributed Tinor's one-time aversion for study was to a deep adolescent crisis. Naturally enough, a homeless orphan had to be shown the right path first of all. Now, since Tinor had been awarded his doctorate with a summa cum laude, he saw the world very differently and it was to be assumed that he was a grown man, who knew what he wanted and what would be best for his further professional career and for Italy. Therefore everyone was secretly quite sure that there was only one city in the world which Tinor could decide upon - Rome.

Chapter 11

"Poison in the hands of a wise man is a remedy; a remedy in the hands of fool is poison."
Giacomo Girolamo Casanova

Very early the next morning Tinor hastily left his little student room visited Doctor Focali who was practicing in a small homeopathic practice in the Old Town area of Naples.

He didn't recognise Tinor at first, it had after all been almost 15 years since he had last seen him as a small child. Yet something about the young man looked familiar to him, maybe it was because he had seen his photo in a newspaper very recently. It might also be the curly red hair, the pale skin, dotted with freckles or the gaunt countenance of the Italian which somehow seemed familiar to Focali. As Tinor introduced himself, Focali stood motionless for a few seconds, but then in his mind's eye he suddenly saw in front of him the sickly, pale young boy in the orphanage, whose malria he had treated at the time.

Focali warmly welcomed the young man and asked him to take a seat opposite his antique writing desk.

"Signor Focali", Tinor hesitated, "I am a man of few words, yet I would like to express a request to you without beating about the bush. I would like to become a homoeopathist; where would you suggest that I do my training?"

Focali was visibly taken aback; after all, one of the youngest physicians in Italy was sitting in front of him, a new genius in the medical skies, as one newspaper had described Tinor – and of all things, he wanted to become a homoeopathist! Focali felt deeply honoured for himself and for his profession.

"I really am delighted", said the homoeopathist, "hand I believe that here in Naples you are in exactly the right place! After all homeopathy had come to Italy in the so-called period of promulgation in 1827, in Hahnemann's lifetime, and it was even said that Naples was the very first city outside of Germany in which the teachings of homeopathy became established. Around 1830 Hahnemann's key students, like the two French men Sébastien Des Guidi and Benoît Mure studied homeopathy here in Naples. It was not until a few years later until information about homeopathy crossed the pond to America. So, why not start training right here in Naples? I can recommend an excellent school to you; indeed you will be aware that any school will welcome you with open arms! I too of course am happy to support you during your training. If you have any questions, you can come to me at any time."

"Tante grazie, signor Focali", replied Tinor, "but I want to go far away from here. Everyone here thinks that they know me, who I am and what I want to do. Strangers have even accosted me in the street asking me for my autograph. What should I say to these people? I don't owe them a thing! I just want to lead my own life in peace, do you understand? And then there is the war in Germany which is troubling me greatly. I want to live in peace. I experienced enough disputes in my childhood to last me a lifetime. We cannot foresee how political events will further develop, but I do not have a good feeling about it. I also think that Italy will be involved in the war. I don't think I want to stay in Europe at all. I want to go to America! Could you recommend me a university there?"

"Ok, young man, I understand what you are saying; even though I am very sorry that you want to leave Italy and Naples in particular, but I can wholly comprehend your reasons and concerns. I am much too old and have been rooted in Naples for too long to even consider setting up a life anywhere else in the world. But you, dear Dr. MùMille, you are young and gifted! Go to New York my dear boy! Homeopathy is experiencing a tremendous upsurge in America at the moment. This is thanks to Doctor Constantin Hering. He was one of the most notable of Hahnemann's pupils and a doctor who was very willing to try out new things. He bequeathed a monumental textbook, the Materia Medica, in ten volumes, which is still one of the best and most complete doctrine of homeopathic medicines."

Focali stood up, went to his big bookcase and stroked Hering's ten-volume work lovingly with is hand. He then continued:

"This outstanding man's enthusiasm went so far that he even acutely poisoned himself with the venom from the Lachesis snake. Yet this scientific martyrdom made it possible for Hering to bring the key concept of nosodes to homeopathy! In homeopathy nosodes are a group of medicines which are manufactured from animal or human material such as blood, secretions or pathogens. But I do not want to take up so much of your time and I don't want to lecture you; you yourself will learn enough about homeopathy! Yes, Tinor, go to America and accept

Hahnemann's legacy! I wish you all the very best. And you do of course know where you can find me should you ever need my help. But before I forget – when you are across the pond, remember to visit the memorial to Hahnemann in Washington! It was inaugurated over 40 years ago and is the biggest memorial to Hahnemann in the world – very impressive! Buon viaggio!"

Tinor gratefully took the piece of paper on which Focali had written the address of the New York university and bid farewell silently with a gracious handshake.

Chapter 12

"If someone calls themselves a homoeopathist, he can practice homeopathy and nothing else; if one acknowledges the law of similitude, one has no choice!"
Adolf zur Lippe

Bewilderment and consternation spread when Tinor's mentors and professors learned that their pupil wanted to become a homoeopathist. How could something like that happen? In their eyes homeopathy was nothing more than pure charlatanry using placebos – a healing method which could only become established due to people's ignorance and gullibility! Monsignore Ronca was indeed aware of Tinor's healing by the knowledgeable homeopathic doctor Focali, but that might also have been mere chance; Tinor mustn't become a homoeopathist himself! He, Umberto Ronca, was as a child also in the travelling circus – and he had been very taken with it – nonetheless, he hadn't become a clown for goodness sake! Why did this young wonder doctor want to squander his talents – the man with the golden hands; whom any clinic would have been happy to brag about having in their operating theatre? Why did Tinor want to heal in the shadows of mainstream, traditional medicine, when he would be able to stand in the light, in the spotlight of the world? His pupil wanted to become a shadow healer!

Regardless of the opinion of others, the same day that he had visited Focali, Tinor withdrew money from his account in the Banca di Napoli, which he had earned at the hospital as a surgical assistant. He then went to the port and at the ticket desk purchased a ticket for the Napoli – Genoa – New York crossing for the day after next.

Back in the student residence, the young doctor stuffed his few possessions into a suitcase and ran all kinds of errands to get ready for his trip, since he wanted to spend the next day alone. Tinor wanted to bid farewell to his homeland, which he might never see again.

First thing in the morning the next day, at eight o'clock, when the heat had not yet hit the vibrant city of Naples with all its might, Tinor went to the station and got on the bus to Valle di Pompeii.

Even though he had not been there for many years, not much had changed in his little hamlet. Time did not seem to have left its mark here. Just like hundreds of years ago, children played barefoot on the piazza and reverent pilgrims knelt and kissed the stone steps outside the portal of the pilgrimage church of Madonna of the Rosary. Tinor too went back into the church, knelt at the altar in front of the picture of the Virgin Mary as he had done in bygone days and prayed quietly:

"Do you see that I am now fulfilling my promise that I made to you many, many years ago – I am becoming a homoeopathist!"

It looked as if the Madonna was smiling at him.

Afterwards Tinor visited the orphanage where he had spent so many years of his childhood to say his goodbyes. But he didn't meet Monsignore Ronca – who had already been commandeered to Rome. Tinor was delighted that Ronca's great dream of an ecclesiastical career in the Vatican seemed to have been fulfilled. Sister Giulia had already died, shortly after Tinor had started his medical studies; other than them, there was no-one else in the orphanage with whom Tinor had had heartfelt personal contact.

He strolled alone like a stranger among strangers around the orphanage, in which he knew the grain of every stone, every step and every scent in the different rooms. After Tinor had said his own goodbyes to Valle di Pompeii, the pilgrimage church and the orphanage, he asked if he could leave his shoes for a few hours at the monastery gateway and collect them in the evening.

Barefoot, just as in his childhood, Tinor now walked on the old familiar path along the coast to his home town of Resina. It might be the last time in his life that he would smell the scent of lemon and orange blossoms and that his gaze would be drawn to the azure blue sea in front of the rugged rocky Sorrento Peninsula. Just as he had done when he was a child, he tried to soak up every second of these precious moments, with every pore of his being and to store it in all the cells in his body for ever more.

Soaked with sweat, he finally reached his childhood home that he not set foot in, in the last fifteen years.

In the intervening period the old Roman city of Herculaneum beneath the house had been almost completely uncovered. Apart from that, time seemed to have stood still in this little southern Italian village too. Hoards of children were running barefoot, screaming wildly, through the narrow alleys, in which washing was hanging between the houses. Skinny cats roamed through the area, always on the look-out for a tasty morsel. Here and there was an old lady, dressed in black, sitting outside her humble dwelling, seemingly absorbed in some handcraft. As ever, his old neighbour Gilda was also sitting there. Next to her front door hung an old, rusty bird cage with a canary, which let out a soft 'cheep' now and then. When she caught sight of Tinor, a brief memory from the past flashed over her old face, but Gilda was now too old and had become too weary to give any further thought to the MùMilles.

When Tinor arrived at the house of his hard childhood days, he knocked at the wooden front door, but no-one seemed to be there. The dated nameplate was still on the door. Even after knocking several times, nobody opened. Tinor took an envelope from his trouser pocket, in which he had out some money and on which he had written, "For Lucia". On the back he had written, "Amore, vado in America. Forse ci vediamo un'altra volta. Tuo fratello Tinor." He then tucked the envelope between the door and the doorframe and took the same route back to Valle di Pompeii, to collect his shoes from the orphanage.

Chapter 13

"In order to heal gently, quickly, certainly and lastingly, choose in every case of illness a medication which can activate a similar ailment!"
Samuel Hahnemann

Tinor was standing at the bow of the steamer, when the Seastar III came within sight of New York harbour on the evening of 5th October 1941. The gaunt Italian, who had set out from the sweltering heat of Naples a few weeks before, was shivering. A harsh wind was blowing on deck, and dusk had already descended. Yet it was not just the unusually cold temperatures which sent shivers down his spine, rather it was the strange celebratory atmosphere of the over 2000 people on board. For the majority of them, the sight of the impressive Statue of Liberty really did stand for freedom and life, since they had managed to escape the war in Europe. Many of the passengers on board were Jews. Only a few German and Italian gentiles were among them, who at the time had the money and the foresight to escape the impending inferno of the war in Europe. Many people were throwing their arms around one another, kissing with joy, weeping freely. Little children watched their parents' paroxysm of joy in bewilderment. It was only much later that they understood that this sight of the Statue of Liberty and a new life in America, was a privilege which had been bestowed upon very few.

Tinor lodged in a small hall of residence close to the Homeopathic University of New York. The name 'University' was of course somewhat exaggerated for the set-up at the time, since the university building was merely a humble New York town house, whose living spaces had been reconstructed into small lecture halls and seminar rooms. But nonetheless, lectures of international capacities in the domain of homeopathy were held in these meagre rooms.

In the university Dr. MùMille was received by the students and lecturers alike with great deference and reverence, since his reputation as an über-talented man in this new realm had spread with lightning speed. That was why it had been easy for Focali to obtain a scholarship for Tinor at the Homeopathic University of New York.

Tinor remained wholly unimpressed by the city itself and the vibrant life and the goings-on around him. What he constantly missed, was not people, but his beloved nature. After all, Tinor also did not know any different in his short life. He did not know what it was like to have friends. He did not know what it is like to really be loved. And he did not know what was like to be in love, or to love. So it really didn't mean that much to him that his contact with his fellow students was very much stand-offish here too. Tinor lived as he always had done since his childhood, completely alone and withdrawn from the world, in his little student room that he only left to go to university, buy books or when the refrigerator was completely empty.

Tinor probably noticed the suspicious looks which his fellow students gave him every day during lectures. He sensed that he was being observed and scrutinised by the others and felt their bewilderment since this misfit, who was the same age as they were, with his curly shock of hair, and who always wore suits a size too big for him which hung limply on his gaunt body, could not be pigeonholed. Their attempt to categorise Tinor somewhere, almost turned into a sort of fear of him, in many of his peers. It was clear for everyone to see that there was genius inside this Italian man; even though Tinor always appeared extremely modest and only ever contributed something to the lectures when he was prompted by a lecturer. The other students were aware too of course that their peer had completed his medical studies with a summa cum laude and was said to have a command of seven foreign languages – among them four ancient languages. So it was not long before this gawky, red-head became the number one topic of conversation at this university too.

Many years later a former student at the Homeopathic University of New York, Englishman Keith Mulligan, described his acquaintance with Dr. MùMille to a colleague thus: "To be honest, meeting MùMille really was very strange. At first I didn't know at all what to make of him. Here came a fully-fledged doctor from Italy to our little university, who had even been conferred a summa cum laude. Of course none of the students at the time were doctors at the time! Out of sheer reverence we didn't even have the courage to speak to him. And since MùMille was a private individual and rarely said anything, we students secretly nicknamed him "the mute". When MùMille went along the corridor, you couldn't even hear his steps. The silent, modest manner of his demeanour had an air of arrogance to us; it was as if he actually wanted nothing at all to do with us. As a result, just like the others, I too did not develop any personal relationship with him; none of us had ever visited him in his digs or even went out for a drink with him. Now, so many years later, that is something I very much regret. But everyone knows what it's like when you're young and you belong to a certain circle of friends. An outsider has no hope there."

Chapter 14

"The simile principle is a sacred archetypal phenomenon of our being."
Herbert Fritsche

This highly gifted man soon began to tire of what was offered to him during the day at university, and so, using his photographic memory, Tinor began to internalise all the pharmacological homeopathic works at night. After studying Hahnemann's "Organon of Medicine" and his Materia medica "Pure Pharmacology", Tinor started on the ten-volume work, "Guiding Symptoms", by German doctor Constantin Hering, written in 1879. Focali had already told Tinor something about this pupil of Hahnemann's. Hering had settled in Philadelphia in 1833 and founded the Hahnemann Medical College and Hospital there. This school then produced the first major generation of American homoeopathists. Tinor continued his studies with works by Hering's pupils – first of all delving into the Materia medica by Timothy F. Allen, then into H. C. Allen's Materia medica of the Nosodes. He then internalised a comprehensive standard reference in homeopathy, which was 2000 pages in length and which is still valid today, "J. T. Kents Repertorium", outlining the most diverse symptoms of disease, and providing a head-to-toe schematic for finding the suitable homeopathic medicine for the disease – the simile – which fit like a key in a lock.

During his time in New York these pharmacologies became a sort of replacement of nature for Tinor, something which he missed so much. The extensive tomes contained descriptions of all the physical and mental symptoms which healing plants, minerals and substances from the animal kingdom could trigger if they were administered to healthy people. And so Tinor not only gained deeply rooted knowledge about the pure guiding symptoms, he also became specifically interested in the "signature" of a plant too. He learned the fundamentals about this in the works by Philippus Theophrastus Aureolus Bombastus von Hohenheim, also known as Paracelsus. Tinor quickly recognised a pioneer in the homeopathic concept in this Swiss doctor and alchemist, since Paracelsus let himself be guided by choosing similitudes. He studied plant signatures and made them the criteria in choosing medication. Tinor was fascinated by the fact that this scholar was aware, even in the 16th century, that Hypericum perforatum – St. John's Wort - for instance, was a medium suitable for wound healing, since the conspicuously large oil glands on the plant's leaves were similar to the pores on human skin. Even through its external appearance a plant provided clues to its healing effect in the human body – simple and ingenious in equal measure! Concerning the doctrine of signatures founded by Paracelsus, the Master himself said,

"You know through the art of the signature how each object is depicted, what it is from and what it belongs to; how the same will always be found, that the art of the signature reveals something which every doctor ought to be able to understand"

As if spellbound, in the nights which followed Tinor studied all the works of Paracelsus. He immediately recognised that the three attributes of a complete homoeopathist had joined forces in him - Paracelsus was a teacher, a clinician and a therapist. He understood how to correctly evaluate, on all levels, the external and the internal; general and specific properties.

His methods of relating his observations in nature to the human body, had mesmerised Tinor from the very first moment; indeed, in every cell of his body he sensed an invisible resonance with Paracelsus' works and ideas – a sort of spiritual blood brotherhood. It was this palpable vibrancy which now explained to him how, during the raising of his own consciousness as a young boy he had felt magically drawn to all plants and growing things.

Tinor pursued the thought that his path through life might have been predetermined from the start. Like a straight line running from A to B. To be sure, anyone who had dedicated themselves to homeopathy, really didn't have any other options to choose. It was also presumably no coincidence that it was a homeopathic medication which had saved his life as a child.

It has to be like this, he thought, when you pursue a vocation. And in Paracelsus, MùMille now found his master, who until now had put the unspoken into words, and whose thoughts fit into Tinor's inner concepts like missing pieces of a jigsaw; completing them to perfection.

By contrast, Samuel Hahnemann had not at all seen his master in Paracelsus; he had even wholly rejected him, even though Paracelsus was not only very similar to him in being and in spirit, but also because their physical stature was also very similar. Natural healers even say that Hahnemann was the embodiment of Paracelsus, who

proved in experiments that he was the reincarnation of
Samuel Hahnemann, through his knowledge of the simile
– the treatment which was most similar to the disorder.
Maybe Hahnemann was, so to speak, a greater power of
Paracelsus, conjectured Tinor. Might it also be that there
was actually a sort of beam of light, a kind of energetic
connection between all the outstanding healers and
homeopaths in this world; a sort of invisible law of
similarity which had been woven through the different
centuries? Maybe the prominent healers of all the eras
were also a kind of simile of one another?

This kind of philosophical thought enabled Tinor to
digress from his own studies and on many evenings his
sense of time and space slipped. He then lay numb on his
bed, immersed in a sea of thoughts, which increased so
far into the infinite until he was barely able to grasp
reality. And yet he felt that his path had to take him
somewhere. He then emerged from Never Never Land
back to the here and now, ran both his hands through his
curly locks and delved once again into his studies.
In the material handed down by Paracelsus, Tinor's
particular interest also lay in the theory of the "Quinta
essentia". This was how Paracelsus described the
spiritual force which was inherent in a plant, a mineral,
an animal or person – its world spirit; its world energy. In
plants, quintessence is revealed in their vegetative power;
in a mineral in its geometric structure; in an animal in its
sentience and in people in their consciousness. Paracelsus
recognised that a medication was merely the carrier of
astral energy, which held the Quinta essentia.
The deeper the insights Tinor gained into the spiritual

legacies and realms of Paracelsus, who was also an astrologer, magician and theologian, the clearer he recognised in himself the spiritual pioneer Hahnemann; and Tinor became ever more certain that there must have been some sort of connection between the two healers. For, just like Hahnemann, Paracelsus, in creating remedies, also endeavoured to eliminate ad infinitum what was injurious to the person, to extract the spirit from it and find a suitable carrier to convey the Quinta essentia, without reducing the effectiveness of the medication. Yet the master did not succeed in all this; death befell Paracelsus early – just like Hahnemann, this alchemist carried out many experiments on himself, indeed the last stage in the making of homeopathic remedies – potentiating – was his reserve. Paracelsus died from lead poisoning, when experimenting on himself, in an attempt to cure an ear infection; the dose he administered to himself was too high.

It was only around 300 years later using the technique of potentiation that Hahnemann succeeded in transporting the Quinta essentia in a dose which was tolerable, when, while experimenting on himself, he potentiated china-bark, a medium to counter malaria. It was thus that the foundation stone of homeopathy was laid.

Chapter 15

"The entirety of the symptoms, this exterior reflection of the inner essence of the illness, is the most fundamental and the sole feature, whereby it can be determined by the illness which cure is required."
Samuel Hahnemann

On account of his intense studying, Tinor quickly advanced to become one of the most outstanding theorists of homeopathic teachings, and in contrast to his fellow students, he didn't have to look for long and repertorise, to find the simile. His mental capabilities to spontaneously grasp all the knowledge he had learned, coupled with the intuition of an introvert, who seemed to be in a position to tap into all his mental sources with his consciousness, bestowed upon Tinor undreamt-of possibilities. When in lectures case descriptions of patients were being discussed, the other students had, mostly, to spend the whole day repertorising and making long lists with cures which might be suitable – the students weighed up all the illness symptoms according to their severity and in a head-to-toe schematic, as they had been taught. They, by the pageful, then wrote out the suitable cure for each symptom from "Kents Repertorium", to finally come to a single result through the most accordances – to the simile. The students struggled all day long to find the right cure, pondered and discussed with one another and with their lecturers.

Tinor did not need to do any such thing. In a matter of seconds he was able to determine the simile, with a 100 per cent success rate. It was like a brainwave that MùMille immediately became aware of the name of the right remedy, in the optimum potentiation level. As if there was no time and no space. His brain seemingly collated in a fraction of a second all the illness symptoms with all the familiar remedy pictures.

Of course the other students found this exceptionally frustrating; they had to stick to the precise procedures which homeopathic expert Herbert Fritsche exactly described – "The homeopathic therapist has to treat a pharmacology – the book in which these are noted – like the Roman priest treats his breviary. Several times a day, always beginning at the beginning and after a few weeks culminating with the final cure, which has a connection with the first; this individual remedy is to be committed (to memory) and retained (making it appear to the world outside that you are meditating); thus bringing it to life. These are the vital exercitia spiritualia; this is the yoga of the homeopathic therapist."

And Tinor quickly achieved the level of master in this Yoga. In spite of the suspiciousness which he encountered time and again, in the second year of his studies it was a frequent occurrence for one of his fellow students and sometimes even already practicing, long-established homoeopathists, to come to him, or write to him looking for advice. Tinor could help them in difficult cases to find the most similar cure, the simile.

Tinor's fellow student Keith Mulligan also said later:
"We were really fed up with him. But we couldn't deny that the mute was a genius. He was never once wrong when it came to finding a simile."

It wasn't long before Tinor was asked by the university management at the time, to give talks about individual topics. In a few months Tinor became the most respected lecturer in the university – even though he was still as student himself. His lectures about individual cures such as Hypericum perforatum, St John's Wort, and about the snake venom Lachesis and the nature of nosodes were very well attended.

Fewer attended lectures when Tinor spoke about the philosophy of homeopathy and about his favourite topic, the law of similarity, since as soon as Tinor took to philosophical terrain, the majority of his audience were not in a position to follow his complex, intellectual interpretations and a few, even though they had a high regard for his qualities as a homoeopathist, secretly thought that he was a fantasist, or just a complete crackpot, who was sure to go cuckoo.

Astonishingly, Tinor simply set aside his shyness at the start of every lecture at the lectern. Beyond his audience, beyond time and space, MùMille immersed himself in an intellectual flight of fancy in the healing art of homeopathy and let himself be carried off by his own monologue, right through space and time, into a sort of philosophical ecstasy:

"... for even in the Mystery of Golgatha the law of homeopathy is reflected, Homoeopathia divina – divine homeopathy. Is it not the law of similarity when God's son is the image of the divine? Is it not the Eucharistic bread, God incarnate, the homeopathic medication, which, when we ingest it, makes us similar to God? He gave us a simile, and at the same time we are the simile

of God! We are his sons and daughters; we are similar to him since he created us as his image. Why did he do that? To heal himself? In a way yes – to understand himself for what he was, the creator. And what would a creator be without creation?..."

Chapter 16

"But medicine is not what the teeth chew; no one can see medicine. It does not lie in the body, it lies in strength."

Paracelsus

In his third and final year of study, Tinor attentively followed the lectures of a guest Dutch lecturer, who moved him very much; indeed, even stirred him up, since he felt that there was a spirit within the Dutchman which was similar to his own in some way.

Roderick van Diljke was, like Tinor, of lean build and was maybe 20 years older than him. His facial expression reflected something of timeless enlightenment, which Tinor found fascinating from the very first moment. Although Roderick's facial features were marked with little wrinkles and the hair on his head consisted only if a little grey semi-circle, extending from one ear to the other, his face radiated a grace, coupled with innocence. He was something of an androgynous being, not quite male, not quite female, which was also highlighted by his delicate voice, which for a man was somewhat too high in pitch.

Holländer's lectures also aroused an interest in Tinor. In the last few years Roderick had busied himself intensely with the topic of the carriers of homeopathic medicine and had also done a lot of his own research. In experimental studies he had demonstrated that a homeopathic medicine changed the structure of the carrier water; indeed, water was, so to speak, a unique example. Homeopathic medicine left its individual mark on the carrier water – for Holländer this was proof that water was transporting individual healing information, the Quinta essentia. The otherwise somewhat taciturn Tinor suddenly felt a considerable urge within him; he definitely wanted to speak with this lecturer in person about his research. When the Dutchman had finished his lecture and was tucking away his manuscript into his leather satchel with his slender hands, Tinor approached the lectern and introduced himself – which had been completely unnecessary, since Roderick had also long since heard about this rare, red-headed doctor, who was rumoured to be able to repertorise accurately, in a matter of seconds.

Even during their initial exchange of worlds, unfamiliar, peculiar feelings arose within Tinor. It was as if he could feel Roderick's subtle bodily vibes. His heart suddenly began to race. It was as if he had found a brother and a friend in Roderick, who had suddenly emerged from nowhere and who was so familiar. A wonderful warm sensation arose in him, until this time this was a sensation about which he had only read in books; and which he did not actually know if it really existed.

Tinor was truly delighted that Roderick understood him, that he also had an interest in chatting to him more extensively.

The two homoeopathists arranged to meet the same evening in MùMille's student residence to continue their intellectual exchange undisturbed and in peace and quiet. Roderick said good-bye to Tinor with an almost tender gesture, as he put his hand on Tinor's upper arm for a few seconds.

Strangely touched by this unaccustomed physical contact, Tinor left the lecture hall.

When Roderick entered the meagre student room in the evening, he embraced Tinor by way of a welcome; something which irritated Tinor greatly, since he did not know whether this sudden invasion of his private sphere, into his personal aura and space, was something that he was happy with. In any case, it confused him greatly. Nonetheless with this embrace Tinor was able to feel what an exceptionally sensitive being he held in his arms; he sensed that Roderick, as though he were made out of the finest porcelain, was vulnerable; indeed this man felt almost ethereal.

The two homoeopathists then sat down at the little wooden table by the window. They remained in silence for the first few minutes. It seemed like neither of them dared utter the first word to break the divine silence. It was as if an intense meeting of two emotional people had overpowered them and they both needed a bit of time to take in that it might well be that two kindred spirits had met. Eventually it was Roderick who was the first to break the silence:

"Tinor, I think you know what I am feeling and I know that you feel it too. I don't need to beat around the bush and anyway, I don't much go in for small talk. I have never in my life met a person to whom I have felt so drawn from the very first moment. I believe you feel that it is the same for me. Even as a child I always wanted to find a friend, someone who thought and felt like I did; a blood-brother. I am now almost forty, but it's never too late! I think that in you I have found a friend, more even, that I have found a spiritual brother – which is why I want to speak quite directly with you. My stay in New York is drawing to an end, the day after tomorrow I take a flight back to Amsterdam. I don't have much more time here. So I would like to ask you straight out and without any convolution – will you come with me to Amsterdam? I live in a modest terrace house in the inner city area, where I carry out my homeopathic research and have set up a small practice. My home is not large, but there is enough room for two. And Amsterdam – well, in comparison to New York isn't exactly the hub of the universe – but you will see that it is a city of great freedom and tolerance. Everyone there can live as they please; I am sure you will like it."

Bewildered, Tinor looked into Roderick's blue-grey eyes. What did fate have in store for him? Why go to Amsterdam? How could an encounter set the points of your life in a completely new direction within a few seconds? Roderick returned Tinor's gaze gently and calmly. He had already anticipated that Tinor would say no. After a while Tinor replied: "I will have finished my studies here in two semesters; please expect me in Amsterdam then."

Chapter 17

"In the Christian model, functioning homeopathy
begins with charity, a propos healing."
Herbert Fritsche

A week before completing his homeopathy studies,
Tinor received news that his parents had died
unexpectedly. After his father Alfonso succumbed to
serious inflammation of the lungs, Concetta then
followed him to the grave two weeks later. As Tinor
discovered in a letter from his sister Lucia, Concetta had
not recovered from Alfonso's death and one morning
when Lucia went to visit her mother, she had found
Concetta dead in bed.

Due to these events, Tinor decided to visit his sister
Lucia in Italy before his planned trip to Amsterdam.

When the lecturers at the Homeopathic University
heard that Tinor was to leave New York in the next few
days, he experienced a similar wave of consternation as
he had done when he decided to leave Italy after his
medical studies.

All the lecturers were deeply distraught since
someone like Tinor, who repertorised like a master and
who internalised over 3000 images of remedies and had
an instant recall memory, was someone who they would
only let of under protest. Of course the university would
have felt very honoured if Tinor were to have stayed as a
lecturer, or even as a principal.

One or another of the lecturers had even secretly
hoped to be able to open up a joint clinic with Tinor in
New York, since after all this Italian doctor and

homoeopathist would also be a sure thing for a very flourishing business.

Lucia was the only one of Tinor's sisters who still lived in Resina. His other sisters had in the meantime all married and moved to Italy's economically better-off north. They lived there with their families, dispersed between Bolzano, Milan and Padua. From what Tinor was able to intimate from Lucia, the MùMille's family tradition lived on, for all the sisters had to a greater or lesser extent, married thuggish men.

Lucia too had married and now lived with husband Giancarlo and their three children in Tinor's former parental home in Resina. Yet Tinor was barely able to sense his earlier inner bonds with Lucia when he visited. Lucia now had a family of her own and her own life, and she had buried the memories of her big brother somewhere deep in her heart, that time when Monsignore Umberto Ronca had come and just took Tinor with him. Lucia had been very happy when, one summer evening, she had met Giancarlo at the beach and they had quickly decided to get married; it was a great reason to finally break away from her family, initially moving in with her husband and his mother. Their wedding finally detached her from the peculiar surname MùMille too; she also believed that in so doing she would also be able to cast off the tragic experiences of her childhood by taking on her husband's typically Italian surname, Magnano.

Giancarlo Magnano begrudgingly accommodated Tinor as a guest in the house which was now his home. He had also one of the wild group of children in Resina who had derided and spat at the red-headed misfit. Maybe he feared that Tinor, the only male descendent of the MùMilles, had only come to parade himself as the legal heir to this house. That was why Giancarlo distanced himself from Tinor and also tried to give his wife no opportunity whatever to speak with Tinor alone. In a certain way he seemed to be jealous of Tinor; for once – in a moment of weakness –Lucia recounted to him, in tears, about the special relationship she had had with her big brother in her childhood. Although she never actually told Giancarlo what had actually happened in the MùMille household. Giancarlo would certainly never have married her if had found out how Lucia from an early age had to tacitly fulfil Alfonso's desires. It was Giancarlo's desires which she tacitly fulfilled, and it was not difficult for Tinor to recognise Lucia's silent suffering. He wanted to help his sister, but she didn't allow him; she never wanted to be reminded about the events of her childhood in her life again. Even seeing Tinor again, she was confronted with an indefinable dark shadow, which she refused to believe, let alone face. Of course Tinor would have been able to administer his sister a homeopathic dose to heal the shade of the past using a simile. But Lucia didn't want to take any medication from her brother, not less one such as that. Lucia's behaviour and Giancarlo's hostile approach to Tinor lead him to only spend a few days in Resina and from then on to have no further contact with Lucia, so as not to bring about a collapse of the facade of her domestic harmony.

On his final day in Italy Tinor was again magically drawn to the pilgrimage church of the Madonna of the Rosary in Valle di Pompeii. He reverently entered the nave, heavy with the scent of incense, crossed himself and knelt, just as he had done as a child, in front of the famous picture of the Virgin Mary and prayed:

"Holy Mother of God, I have now become a homeopathist, just as I had promised you, but I have not found love. Please tell me how I can find love if I am never able to share myself? It is only now that I can grasp what happened to me in my childhood and I have now even lost Lucia, my only love. How can I become a good homoeopathist if I have no altruism? How can I become a good person if there is an absence of love in my life?"

And for the first time in many years, Tinor was overcome by deep sobbing; he could do nothing else than let these tears run freely in this church which had become so dear to him.

When he was about to stand up from his supplication, a Father was suddenly standing behind him; he had noticed Tinor's tears. He lay a hand on Tinor's shoulder, and looking at his distraught face, said to him:

"Never give up. All of our lives we strive for salvation. But keep in mind the secret of alchemy – for two substances to be able to melt and become one, a third element is always needed. Love."

And with an enlightened smile the Father added, "Ma amore sempre c'è – love is everywhere."

Without any further farewell, the clergyman turned away from Tinor with a spring in his step and disappeared into the rear area of the church. His words resonated in Tinor's innermost being for a long time:

Amore sempre c'è.

Chapter 18

"...the nose and respiratory organs are excellently responsive to the effect of medications in liquid form; through smell and through breathing in through the mouth. Yet it is also the entire, remaining parts of our bodies covered with skin which are proficient in the taking in the effect of solutions, in particular when rubbing in is carried out concurrently with this intake."
Samuel Hahnemann

Roderick's "residence – cum practice – cum laboratory" was located at a small canal in an established inner city district in Amsterdam, over which the melancholy of the old port town was palpable in the air. The laboratory was in the cellar of the narrow terraced house, the practice was on the ground floor and his living area took up both upper floors.

Tinor felt relatively good in Amsterdam, at least his somewhat Nordic appearance didn't cause much of a stir as it had done in the south of Italy, even though in Amsterdam too he lead a shadowy existence, spending the majority of his time with Roderick in the laboratory in the cellar. It was only curiosity which drove him out of the house now and then. Together, the two homoeopathists then went in search of old books about healing plants and about the history of medicine and homeopathy, in the nearby antiques quarter on the Spiegelgracht. Tinor fervently rummaged around in the dusty antiques until he eventually found a new item to assuage his hunger for intellectual nourishment. His reputation as a highly talented individual quickly spread with his relocation to Amsterdam and Tinor relished the fact that he was finally able to live in long yearned-for anonymity in this multi-cultural society. Over two thirds of all of Amsterdam's inhabitants were not Dutch; rather they came from all corners of the earth. Here, no-one was in the slightest bit interested in Tinor MùMille.

Whereas Roderick continued with his research about the carrier, water, Tinor's point of focus lay in the administration of a homeopathic medicine. He used Roderick as a guinea pig; Tinor tested the effect and every conceivable way of administering a variety of remedies
on him.

Since Tinor's arrival Roderick was literally flourishing. He loved Tinor, almost idolized him, was subservient to him, hung on the genius' every word and was delighted with all the homeopathic experiments which Tinor carried out on him. With great delight he submitted himself to all the test remedies and also tried to surmise Tinor's desires. But Tinor had no desires. The world outside was too foreign to him. He was just satisfied, that he was simply able to pursue his studies in peace and quiet. He also wasn't actually altogether certain whether Roderick did love him. The Dutchman had indeed become a close friend to him, a kindred spirit – Roderick was every bit as fantastic a homoeopathist and scientist as he was himself – but whether that was love, Tinor was not in a position to say. In contrast, Roderick surrendered himself yearningly and devotedly to his love, even if Tinor were not himself able to reciprocate it.

In the course of time Tinor's methods of administering medications had become even more subtle. He rubbed just a few drops on to Roderick's wrist, had him merely sniff in a little bottle, placed some on his bedside table or rubbed a homeopathic remedy into specific parts of his body. Sometimes he merely wrote the name of a preparation on a piece of paper, placed this under Roderick's pillow and observed whether Roderick had any dreams or physical reactions. Tinor then exactly recorded all of Roderick's symptoms which had been triggered by the medication and compared them in a matter of seconds with the guiding symptoms of various editions of the Materia medica. During this meticulous work, which Tinor carried out over many decades with a great deal of passion, he determined that even for the most subtle administration, for instance, when he only called out the level of potentiation of the homeopathic cure to Roderick in passing; he was conveying the Quinta essentia, the healing information to Roderick– it was no wonder then that eventually Roderick was influenced by this exceptional subtleness and sensitivity. This became especially clear to Tinor when a cure was rubbed on to the wrist, directly on the artery - right on the point on which life perceptibly pulsed. As a result Tinor then meticulously experimented in the next few years with this specific way of administering medication.

Chapter 19

"For when nature makes copper from iron and gemstones from liquids, she can do even more with her latent powerful forces."
Paracelsus

After a few years of researching and countless self-experiments, Tinor dedicated himself with increasing interest to the group of medicines known as nosodes, the potentiated preparation of pathogens and secretions. After he had tested the most current nosodes on himself and on Roderick, with the most important, Lachesis, the snake venom from the South American bushmaster, leading the way, the doctor and homoeopathist finally found the time, to get to grips with another interesting original edition of a medieval work about the history of medicine. It concerned a treatise about "Theriac", a medical concoction which had been mentioned time and again over many centuries since ancient times, and which was regarded as a panacea.

One single medicine for all illnesses – this thought fascinated Tinor on the one hand, yet on the other, what substance or power of nature did such a mighty healing power have? In one of the second-hand bookshops at Amsterdam's Spiegelgracht he had recently been passed this very rare copy of a book "de salvia divina"– "about the divine art of healing" – by a very old antiquarian bookseller. In total only four volumes of this valuable medical-historical work had been published, and it was neither known who the author of this wonderful work was, nor who owned the other three original editions. It was assumed that two of the copies no longer existed, since they would have been destroyed in the time of the Inquisition due to their heretical content. Tinor now held one edition in his hands, the other edition might possibly have been under lock and key in the catacombs at the Vatican.

When Tinor had been standing at the bookshelf in the second-hand bookshop and was taking an interest in the six-volume original edition by Paracelsus, the homoeopathist suddenly got the feeling that the antiquarian bookseller's eyes were virtually boring into his back. He then turned around to the white-haired book-dealer and gave him a questioning look. However, he did not desist from his piercing gaze and looked Tinor right in the eye for a while, without saying a thing. He then suddenly pulled out an old book from under the counter, which as well as handwritten recipes, also contained exact anatomical descriptions of human organs and tissues as well as diagrams of various healing plants.

"This book contains knowledge", coughed the old man, "which has long been lost without trace. Contemporary medicine and even the Vatican want to distance themselves from this, and are relieved that the public don't know much about it. But the initiate will find a new way in." Then, looking left and right, he made sure that there was no-one else in the bookshop and gave Tinor the precious copy, without even wanting to take a few guilder for it.

According to this old text, in the early modern medicine of the Middle Ages, people had believed in the healing power of a human substance - a distillate which was obtained from a healthy person had to be a cure for any type of illness - the body of a dead person would only have traces of the original life force of a healthy person - and these could be given to a sick person. Tinor continued reading and discovered that the processing of parts of dead bodies into medicines was even common practice at that time. The executioner counted as medical personnel and had the task of anatomising the executed, as long as they were healthy. Skull, fat, skin and bones – all sorts of tissues were removed by these "medicine suppliers" and further processed by the executioner into expensive medication, especially the already mentioned panacea from ancient times - Theriac, which was frequently mixed with up to fifty other ingredients, among them opium. However the recipes made from human tissues were in no way dealt with in dark, clandestine channels; rather they were openly offered for sale in pharmacies and were recommended by many doctors for all sorts of ailments.

After reading this odd medical history work Tinor fell into a kind of half-sleep in his old easy chair. His last conscious thought was of San Gennaro, the patron saint of Naples, whose blood had been collected after his beheading. After Tinor awakened again from this short snooze, he chatted to Roderick about this secret book, the "salvia divina", and could rid himself of the thought of Theriac.

Presumably also due his feeling of solidarity, Roderick suddenly had a new idea for a new self-experiment - a joint nosode using his and Tinor's blood!

Tinor complied with Roderick's wish, and took a few drops of blood from himself and from Roderick and potentiated from this mix the "van Diljke-MùMille nosode" up to a one thousand potency – a task which took several days and nights. Then both homoeopathists each took a few drops of this nosode, to merge their spiritual blood-brothership with one another and to bring together their ideas and knowledge about homeopathy into one common spirit and to let this live on should one of them die.

Quite in contrast to homeopathic research, which, just like potentiation levels went on ad infinitum, the homeopathic practice wasn't exactly flourishing. Tinor was not that popular, since it was not possible for this odd homoeopathist to gain the trust of a lot of patients, even though there should have been a long queue of people outside his practice every day, on account of his healing successes. This Italian man in Amsterdam, in his little, cramped consulting room, was much too weird for many people and his reputation as a genius, as the youngest Italian doctor of all time, had vanished after the many years in Amsterdam. When he was consulted by a patient, he did indeed take the patient's history and asked a few strange questions – but otherwise he remained silent. He lacked the jovial, trustworthy aura of a doctor who welcomed a patient with a handshake and immediately enquired in a fatherly and attentive manner about their well-being.

Tinor himself did not like the role of doctor and practitioner. He had always had a certain shyness and even an aversion for people he did not know. Superfluous words were an anathema to him, a waste of valuable energy and practice didn't make it any easier for him. He also had always regarded his focus as being on

intellectual research. Working with patients was something, as far as he was concerned, which was to be done by others; others
who had more life experience than he did. Others who knew what love was.

Even Roderick could not get excited about a lively throng of patients. This androgynous man predominantly attracted exactly the same patients - social outsiders who felt better protected in the care of another outsider, than in a standard doctor's practice; so his patient base included predominantly people without any residence permits, drug addicts and transsexuals.

Thanks to an inheritance which Roderick had received in early adulthood after the death of his parents, he had a financial cushion and did not depend upon the income of the practice alone. That he also shared everything he had with Tinor was just a matter of course for him. Both homoeopathists had no regard for money, commercial thought or for material possessions. To them the mundane was much too far from the cosmos of homeopathy, in which they both lived.

Chapter 20

"It was high time that he (God) let homeopathy be discovered."
Samuel Hahnemann

For almost forty years, Tinor and Roderick lived and researched together in this terraced house in Amsterdam. Four decades in which the two lived out unconditionally their passion for homeopathy.

Roderick, in spite of advanced age, was in the very best of health, and Tinor too, at around 65 years old was fit and well. In the interim, his research in the area of the administration of medicines had bestowed upon him international fame as a leading homoeopathist, in particular on account of the method named after him, MùMille's "Homeopathic Pulsation".

Tinor had discovered and demonstrated in clinical experiments that this kind of administration of tablets, globules and the intake of liquid medicines for specific ailments was vastly superior, since they were applied directly to a living pulse. What could be more obvious that conveying the Quinta essentia right where the pulse of life beats rhythmically, with the vibration then conveying this healing information throughout the body? As simple as the method appeared, it was seminal - with MùMille's homeopathic pulsation the healer trickled the homeopathic remedy onto a sort of sticking plaster and stuck it on to the inside area of the patient's left wrist, right on the artery, for a few minutes, a few hours or days.

Many contemporary homoeopathists from all over the world corresponded with Tinor MùMille, even the new Director of the recently built Homeopathic University of New York, the Croat Dr. Nikola Milec. In a letter he congratulated Tinor on his idea which revolutionised homeopathy.

Dear Dr. MùMille,

As the new Director of the Homeopathic University I have of course heard a great deal about you, your time as a student here with us in New York and your decades of research. I now feel a sense of security that you have further developed homeopathy following in the tradition of Hahnemann with your method of homeopathic pulsation! Of course, not all homoeopathists, who cling to Hahnemann's words like a fly clings to the light, are pleased with your new theory. But you yourself know very well that there are always critics everywhere; pay no attention to their hostilities!

Serving the patient and exploratory healing which becomes apparent to us every day, is much more important; your new method of administering medication using little plasters works very well indeed. I would be delighted to get to know you in person and to welcome you here as a guest lecturer. Let me know when you might be coming back to New York, you are cordially welcome here any time,

Yours, Nikola Milec

Success slowly set in, in the little homeopathic practice in Amsterdam too since the time that Tinor had been doing treatments with the method named after him, and many of his articles had appeared in specialist journals. Although the majority of patients did not get on with Tinor MùMille as a person and found him to be somewhat disagreeable, homeopathy had since become established as an almost approved healing method in Europe and patients now trusted Tinor's new method of administering medication via the skin. For many it was the last-ditch rescue attempt where conventional medicine had failed, and for whom there was nothing else that could help them, or that would save them from certain death.

It was with this very thought that the mother of a girl who was seriously ill with cancer came with her daughter one damp, cold November evening to Tinor's practice for the evening surgery. She had nothing more to lose.

Loudly sobbing, the mother explained to Dr. MùMille the fate of her 15 year-old daughter Frederike, who suffered from a rare form of leukaemia and in the eyes of conventional medicine was regarded as being beyond treatment, after two chemotherapy treatments had not had any effect. Homeopathy was the very last hope she still had for her daughter, otherwise she would surely soon die.

Frederike was a delicate girl with a pale, translucent complexion and smooth blonde hair. Wearily, she attended the first consultation between her mother and the homoeopathist.

After an in-depth anamnesis Tinor administered the girl a medication, which he trickled onto a sticking

plaster and attached to the girl's left wrist. He asked
Frederike to visit him once a week.

Since Frederike's first visit Roderick noticed a certain
change in Tinor's demeanour. Roderick suddenly found
him strangely cheerful, a trait which Tinor had never e
throughout the decades. Tinor now almost set about his
work elatedly, especially on the days when he was
expecting Frederike in the practice. Even Frederike felt
especially drawn to Tinor and she had total trust in her
doctor, even though she started to get worse, which Tinor
attributed to the efficacy of his homeopathic medications.
The so-called initial deterioration had occurred. In
contrast, Frederike's mother was more worried than ever
before. She too felt that something was going on, yet it
was only a vague inkling which was not able to explain
further. She only knew that it worried her. She was
worried too that her daughter was looking visibly worse
than the time previous to these strange sticking plasters
being put on her wrist and faint doubt was percolating
within her as to whether she had made the right decision
in entrusting Frederike to the care of this funny oddball
doctor. Certainly she had at first been overjoyed that Dr.
MùMille had even taken her daughter on as a new
patient, but that had now changed.

To the same extent, while Tinor for the first time in
his life seemed to be blossoming, Roderick, who was
now in his late eighties, suddenly lost his vigour, and his
envy of Frederike tore at his heart strings. He had loved
Tinor for almost his entire life and hoped he would open
up to him at some point. Now, in old age, he had to

witness how in Tinor, love for this infirm 15 year-old girl was clearly blossoming; a wholly simple girl, who, as far as he could tell, did not possess any particular spirit.

When Frederike became palpably weaker she was no longer able to visit the practice and asked Dr. MùMille to make house visits from then on. Tinor was fully aware of his responsibility as a doctor and after the initial worsening symptoms had shown no visible momentum in recovery from the medications, he felt certain inside that it was now inevitable it would come to an end. This was not a healing crisis, but the point at which God had sealed a fate, when there was no longer any escape; a point at which his will would be done. He wanted to be a good doctor, homoeopathist and wonder healer, something which was sealed in his fate, something which could not be prevented by human hand.

Chapter 21

"People are the best medicine for one another."
Indian wisdom

When the homoeopathist visited Frederike in her apartment the next day, he was eager to speak with her mother first of all and gently prepare for the fact that death was imminent, so she could accompany Frederike and enable her to have a peaceful and dignified death. She wanted to hear nothing about this and clung hysterically to Tinor, screaming at him, while gesticulating wildly, berating him for being the last hope for her daughter.

Tinor, who felt that time was running away from him, asked to be able to consult Frederike. Reluctantly, the mother let him be alone with her daughter. Tinor sat on Frederike's bed, who lay there like an angel and was sleeping peacefully. When she finally opened her eyes and looked at the doctor, a barely perceptible smile flashed over her face. Too weak to speak, she motioned to him that she wanted him to hold her.

Tinor put his arms around her, sat her up gently in her bed and held her tightly in his arms for a long time. Bliss flowed through him for a moment, which was maybe only a few seconds, but to him it lasted an eternity. He felt Frederike's tender, emaciated body in his arms and love suffused every cell of his body. Tears of emotion welled up in him. It had taken over 60 years until love had revealed itself to him. He wished that he were able to stay like this with Frederike in his arms for ever and ever. She leant her head gently on his shoulder and with one hand stroked his chest, almost as if she wanted to console him on account of her approaching death. Tinor remembered that it had once been similar with his sister Lucia when he had been ill as a child. His little sister sat by his side on his sick bed, holding her big brother in her arms and consoling him. It was now he who was granted with the mercy of solace; he, who actually wanted to give solace!

Yet this moment of bliss didn't last for long; when Frederike's mother suddenly swung open the door to the sick-room, and at what she thought she saw playing out there, filled with rage she tore away the homoeopathist from her daughter's bed and threw him out, under a torrent of loud insults, forbidding him never to set in the apartment again.

Of course Dr. MùMille still wanted to visit Frederike the next day. He knocked at the door but nobody was at home and Tinor knew intuitively, what had happened. A few days later he received news of Frederike's death from the hospital. The child had been administered another dose of chemotherapy, as a result of which she unfortunately died, since she had come to the hospital too late and her condition had already worsened to the point where she didn't survive the toxic medication.

Tinor's sorrow was deep, not just because of Frederike's death, he was mourning much more out of a deep sense of compassion for the girl whom he had very much wanted to be able to go to sleep in peace.

Yet as great as the personal loss was to him, one thing remained for Tinor from this profound experience - love. Frederike had touched a chord in his soul; a chord which Tinor had never previously been aware that actually existed - Amore sempre c'è. Love is everywhere; even where you might least expect it.

Tinor now lovingly cared for Roderick and endeavoured to anticipate this aged man's every wish. Even though he was not able to love him in body, Tinor still felt as though a door which had been previously shut fast, was now wide open – and the key was love.

Roderick appreciatively accepted the sympathetic feelings, deeds and gifts of Tinor, and died a short while later, with various sticking plasters on his wrist, in deep peace.

Tinor, the sole inheritor of Roderick's effects, had to continue the practice alone from then on. Yet the quiet years in which he had been able to devote himself to his research, were now over. Just a few weeks after Frederike's death he received a criminal complaint from her mother which accused him of being guilty of the death of her daughter and a gruelling process against Tinor, which was to last for years, began. The court-appointed medical expert branded him a Charlatan, and the media stirred up the people of Amsterdam, who were otherwise so tolerant, and they now took the same line. Eventually Amsterdam High Court judged that Tinor was henceforth to be stripped of his licence to practice medicine, and from now on he had to relinquish his title of Doctor in the Netherlands, cease any medical duties and close his homeopathic practice immediately.

A column in an Amsterdam tabloid, of which millions of editions were published, read:

Once again the activities of a dubious practicing doctor have been put to an end. What a pity we turned a blind eye to his conduct for so many years! How many patients had to die because they placed their trust in a homoeopathist who trickled ineffective droplets on to a plaster and stuck it on their wrists? How is it even still possible in our modern era for a Charlatan to get rich at the expense of gullible patients using antiquated healing methods like homeopathy – and then not even recoil when it costs a life? How callous must such a doctor be! Research findings do indeed show that a healing effect can be obtained even using placebos, but a seriously ill person ought not to be exposed to such experiments – it could cost them their life as has been emphatically demonstrated in the case of 15-year old Frederike K. That is why at this juncture I would like to quote the words of the victim's desperate mother, "When someone is in need, they clutch at straws and in so doing, completely shut off their brain. My daughter's death is not the fault of Dr. MùMille alone, I too had a part in it because I did not take her back to receive serious mainstream medical treatment straight away. Had she have received chemotherapy just a few weeks earlier, she would have become healthy again and she would still be alive today!"

Tinor's character meant that he had never been reliant upon approval from others. The legal proceedings, the anonymous threatening letters which had been written to him and the crushing articles about him in the press were unable to shake his foundations; what affected him much more was people's stupidity. There were of course a few of Dr. MùMille's patients who still came to him after the legal proceedings, but he was barely able to appreciate their respect.

The withdrawal of his medical licence was like a slap in the face for Tinor; he lost his licence to heal in the Netherlands, the very thing that had driven his life and his desire in the last few years.

The press and the Amsterdam people celebrated the court decision since they had finally revealed a Charlatan, who wanted only to get rich at the cost of the ill. Tinor was certain that a few centuries earlier they would have publicly pilloried, tortured, and stoned him or hung him on the market square amid a baying mob.

On the other hand, Tinor almost felt something of a relief, since he had not originally wanted to practice and be on the front line dealing with patients, he would have preferred to devote himself wholly to his research. So he considered it to be fate, guided and desired by a higher force; that this court ruling would now open up new paths in his life. His only desire had always been that he be able to share the notion of homeopathy and his knowledge about this healing art, so other therapists would be able to heal people.

Just a few weeks after the devastating court decision, Tinor left the Amsterdam townhouse, together with the practice and everything in it to a young doctor – to the people of Amsterdam this was a clear sign of his defeat and of their victory.

Just like before when Tinor had gone to New York, he packed but a few possessions in his case. There was barely anything worldly on which he had set his heart, except for a single letter which he had received from his sister Lucia in those final few years, which had recounted of death and of farewell. Then there was still a photo of

Frederike and an antique wrist watch which Roderick had once given him as a gift upon his arrival in Amsterdam and on whose gold back was engraved, "Similia similibus curentur, for ever, Roderick".

With a small leather case filled with personal effects and clothes, and a few suitcases which contained his homeopathic research documented in writing and the most important fundamental homeopathic works, the homoeopathist left in a taxi on a cold, rainy December evening for Schiphol International Airport, situated far outside the city and upon the plane getting airborne, he bade farewell to Amsterdam for ever.

Chapter 22

"Only the deeply similar truly provokes the similar."
Carl Gustav Carus

Tinor sat quietly and relaxed in the window seat on the KLM flight from Amsterdam to Naples and was looking out at the encompassing skies, on which twilight was falling in play of red-purple. Satisfied, he felt that it has been a good decision to take up Nikola Milec's offer of becoming a lecturer at the Homoepathic University of New York. Tinor was now over seventy but he felt that he still had plenty of time left to take up a teaching post overseas.

Yet what he wanted more than anything initially was to visit his homeland for one last time; to return to the country of his childhood so many decades ago and cast a final glance from the Gulf of Naples to the turquoise blue sea and the flower island of Capri which sat wonderfully enthroned in it.

The plane soon began its final descent and in just a few minutes Tinor would once again feel Italian soil beneath his feet. Melancholic feelings, coupled with excitement, arose in him. Almost long-lost thoughts were revived – back in Italy, his homeland. Tinor was then finally able to make out from the plane window the kilometres of holiday lights which wove around the Gulf of Naples like a cluster of shining stars. As Tinor set foot again on Italian soil after almost half a century, he had to get his bearings initially. Nothing was the same as it had been, everything had changed. Even in the south of Italy time had not stood still, only the heat was the same.

Masses of tourists from all over the world scurried past Tinor in the brightly lit airport building. This frenzy of activity was not for him, it made him almost light-headed. Tinor was very relieved when he saw a few taxis outside the airport building. He got into the first taxi straight away and told the driver the address of his hotel in the centre of Naples.

The closer he came to the Old Town, the greater the traffic chaos. A loud cacophony of car horns alternating with the grating yells of incensed road users. The spirited driving of the taxi driver meant they arrived at the little city hotel, where Tinor had reserved a room for a few nights, in a very short time. His room was on the first floor, facing out on to the street. Tinor opened the door, went in and carefully placed his linen hat, which concealed his thinning hair, on the table and wiped away the beads of sweat from his forehead. He then sat down on the little balcony to recover from the taxing journey. He sat there motionless for a long time und took in the loud night-time activity in Naples. At the same time he soaked in the warm Naples air, an incomparable mixture of exhaust fumes, heat and sea. He could not get enough of it, so unique was the scent of his homeland to him.

Next morning Tinor immediately picked up the telephone and called the Banca di Napoli, where he still had an account and to which he had transferred the full proceeds of the sale of the house in Amsterdam. The homoeopathist got in touch with the property department and instructed them to purchase an apartment in New York for him immediately – preferably that very day – which was close to the Homeopathic University and which had to be located in New York's medical personnel district, since he would shortly be taking up a teaching position there.

He then drank a glass of water, lifted his hat and made his way to see Sergio Focali. A relatively senseless undertaking as Tinor was aware, since Focali must have been over 90 years old, if he was still alive. Yet Tinor had an inner urge, even if he had already died, to find out more about Focali's life or at least something about his death.

Upon arriving at Focali's former practice, Tinor now saw a little tailor's – Focali had presumably been unable to find a suitable successor for his homeopathic practice. A black-haired Neapolitan lady, about 40 years old, was sitting at an old sewing machine in Focali's former practice rooms.

"Buon giorno Signora!", said Tinor, "Do you know anything about the homoeopathist, who used to work in these rooms?"

The seamstress looked up from her sewing machine in surprise and said all she knew was that he had died decades ago, and that his grave was near the sacred San Gennaro cathedral. Tinor thanked her and immediately went in search of the grave.

The graveyard at the cathedral was many centuries old and was very big; Tinor walked between the graves for more than an hour until he finally found Focali's last resting place.

The grave was tended, a fresh bouquet of flowers and a burning red memorial candle were on the gravestone. The following words were carved into the granite stone:

"Sergio Focali, 1898-1976, Homoeopathist."

Below was the inscription:

"My final thanks go to all the great homoeopathists in this world."

Tinor was overwhelmed by emotion; he owed this doctor so much, indeed, he owed him his life. He then felt a sort of weakness come over him – Tinor hadn't even noticed that it was now midday and the sun was burning right down on Naples. Tinor sat himself down on a park bench which was close to the grave, in the shade of some old trees. He rummaged around in the pockets of his jacket for the emergency homeopathic remedy which he always carried with him in a vial and decided to take a dose of Lachesis, to provide speedy assistance for his circulatory insufficiency. He then looked for Lucia's farewell letter in his trouser pocket, which he had received in his darkest time in Amsterdam; a period in his life which was marked by death and parting, when first Frederike died, then Roderick and finally followed by the judgement of the Amsterdam court.

Caro fratello,

I realise I have turned a blind eye to the truth right through my life. And now look where they have brought me! They have put me in the Sanità psychiatric hospital in Naples and are feeding me all sorts of coloured tablets every day. But this is what happens when you always lie about the shadows in the past and act as though nothing has happened.

If you are reading these words, I am no longer alive. I am secretly stashing all these sedatives and sleeping tablets and will take them as soon as I know that this letter has definitely made the outgoing mail. You don't need to get in touch with me anymore, death is a certainty for me but don't worry about me, since when you read these words I will be in a better world!

My big, clever brother, how I have always missed you, my only ally on earth! I was so proud of you. I am proud of you now too because you are a homoeopathist, even though I don't really know what that is.

But I would now like to let you in on a secret since I do not want to take to the grave all the secrets which I have carried around with me all my life. I don't think Alfonso was your real father. Just before Mama died, she kept saying deliriously, "Tell Tinor about the moonlight on Montecassino and that I loved him so very much, so much that it would have cost me my life if I had ever revealed anything about this love to him."

I don't know what that means, but I assume you will find out.

Should I ever come into the world again, wish a better life for me. But I know now that I also have to do something myself for it to be better. Since if you don't face the dark shadows of the past and don't heal, they eventually eat you up.

But there was something good in my life; you. I have always loved you and will always love you, big brother, forever in eternity,

Yours, Lucia

Chapter 23

"Gentle power is great."
Constantin Hering

Tinor's circulatory insufficiency had settled somewhat. He sat, pondering, in the shade of the trees on a park bench and thought for a long time about his little sister, his glimmer of light, and her last words. She had done as she intended; a few days after he received the letter from the Sanità psychiatric hospital, he received news of Lucia's death – heart failure.

The thought that Alfonso was not his biological father, had not especially affected him. To all intents and purposes, he felt the fact that this man had no blood relationship to him, was a relief.

Tinor pored over Lucia's mysterious words time and again, about what might have happened that night on the Montecassino, with whom his mother Concetta had had a little rendezvous, during which he had presumably been conceived. But he would probably never find out.

Completely immersed in his thoughts and ruminations, Tinor sat there for a while until a woman of around the same age approached Focali's grave. Tinor looked at her quizzically.

"I am his daughter, and who are you?", she said as she busily swapped the old bunch of flowers for freshly cut flowers. Tinor stood up and went over to the woman.

"I am a homoeopathist", he replied, "I knew your father and I held him in very high regard. He treated me when I was a child, when I had malaria and he probably saved my life".

The woman stood up in amazement and now looked at him right in the eyes.

"My father told me about you once. He told me just before his death that he had an illegitimate son. He didn't know about it himself for a long time. But one time he had to cover for a doctor in Resina and pay a visit to a gravely ill woman who died shortly afterwards. There he recognised a secret old flame from his younger days – or should I say his youthful indiscretion? – and learned about a son that the pair had conceived. Nobody knew about this or even suspected, Mama neither of course. Are you from Resina?"

With that the woman turned around, without waiting on a reply and disappeared in a labyrinth of gravestones, as quickly and silently as she had arrived. Tinor stood stone-still in front of Focali's grave and tried to collect his thoughts. So his feeling was right after all, he owed his life to Focali in the truest sense of the word!

Confused, but nonetheless relieved, Tinor left the final resting place of this man who presumably was his biological father. The sorrow that in life he had not had a real father-son relationship with this great man, was great, but even greater was his love for Focali, which now germinated in him, just like a new feeling, hitherto unknown - he was proud to be his son.

In the days which followed Tinor undertook a voyage of farewell to the places in his homeland which he loved. As he had done as a child, he visited the pilgrimage church in Valle di Pompeii to the Blessed Virgin and went by taxi to his much loved coast of the Gulf of Naples; it had become too cumbersome for him in his old age to go on foot. Finally he then fulfilled his childhood dream – to see Capri one last time – and then to die. He had never been on the nearby flower island before, he had been unable to fulfil this dream in his austere childhood days.

He then visited the Benedictine monastery near Salerno on the Montecassino and thought about the rendezvous between his mother and his father, the very place it had taken place, where many centuries ago knowledge of Arabian medicine joined western tradition; a spiritual fusion of knowledge and the insight which characterises the history of medicine in Europe to the present day.

Only now, later in life, was it possible for Tinor to better understand his mother. Might she even have really loved Focali at the time? It would not have been possible for her to leave her husband Alfonso. A divorce in Italy in the 1920s would have been unthinkable. Concetta would certainly have had to pay for this move with her life. There was probably nothing left for her to do at the time than to accept her fate and to deny the love which she had felt in reality for this child. And so it was that his mother rejected and hated him– although he was Concetta's only child borne of love.

When Tinor arrived back in his hotel in Naples after a few days, he felt relieved and happy. It was as if the shadows of the past had simply fallen away from him. He had settled everything and had seen his homeland again.

He now fell into a sort of trance-like state. He reviewed his whole life in his mind's eye. Yes, his childhood had not been easy, yet he had achieved what he had wanted to achieve; he had become a homoeopathist and now as a lecturer in New York would be able to pass on all of his knowledge to his students.

Gratefulness, love and a deep inner peace now enveloped him like a protective aura and made his brown eyes sparkle – it was a special kind of sparkle, the kind you only see in older people who have come to terms with their fate, the radiance of an inner display of someone who is cognisant.

The next day Tinor carefully packed up his few possessions, put on his old linen hat and set out on his last big journey, which would take him from Naples via Rome to New York.

Chapter 24

"If a chemist examines a homeopathic remedy, he finds only water and alcohol; if he examines a floppy disc, he finds only iron oxide and vinyl. Yet both can hold any amount of information."

Peter Fisher

At the age of 80 Tinor's face looked like that of a new-born. His skin was wrinkled and waxen and his grey hair and curled wildly here and there above his ears, like the downy fluff of a new-born infant. His head was almost bald; making his intellectual high brow seemed all the more monumental.

That January the rain pounded non-stop for three weeks on the windowpanes of his apartment. Tinor propped himself up on the window ledge and looked down upon the gloomy avenue, on which only cars and umbrellas were to be seen. Diagonally opposite was the New York Memorial Hospital, in whose access road an ambulance was pulling into, sirens wailing loudly.

Tinor turned away from this view, which was the same day in, day out and sat down on his old sofa. With meticulous precision the old man rolled up his left shirt sleeve, bound his arm with a belt and inserted the cannula for an injection. With a purposeful prick Tinor got right into the vein first time, which became accentuated in a blue-yellow hue in the crook in his arm. With his right hand he pulled back the syringe, until it was filled to the half-way point with the dark red blood. He then pulled the needle out of his vein again, syringed the freshly drawn blood into a test tube, stoppled it and carefully labelled it with the date and the time. He placed the blood specimen into a wooden rack on his kitchen table, the round openings of which already contained a whole gamut of labelled test tubes filled with blood.

For a brief moment the aged homoeopathist paused and looked again at the wooden rack which held all the blood samples, as if it were able to tell him something about himself. He whispered quietly, "Similia similibus curentur", and then shuffled in his felt slippers into the hallway. There he put on the only pair of outdoor shoes he owned, took his crumpled coat from its peg, slipped it on awkwardly and put on his old linen hat.

With a final scrutinising glance he made sure that everything was in its rightful place in the kitchen, which had been turned into a laboratory. It was only then that he left his apartment.

It was cold and damp outside. Tinor MùMille pulled up the collar of his coat to his ears to shield himself, walked along the busy avenue, past the giant entrance portal of the New York Memorial Hospital, then turned right and after a few hundred metres reached the wrought-iron gateway to the Homeopathic University of New York.

In the entrance hall he was immediately surrounded by awestruck students who had already been waiting for him and wanted to ask him specific questions. Among the students was Hans Ganter. The 30 year-old had just completed his medical studies in Graz. If there was such a thing as a favourite pupil for Dr. MùMille, then it certainly would be Ganter. Maybe because Tinor had sensed a sort of obsession with homeopathy in the Austrian as was inherent in him and all the great homoeopathists. Hans Ganter was the only student who had ever been in MùMille's apartment and with him had carried out some self-experiments, in keeping with the time he spent in Amsterdam.

Just as with each of his lectures, a large throng of students accompanied the aged homoeopathist up the steps to the already overcrowded lecture hall on the first floor. Among those present was also an interested publisher, who Tinor had spoken with a few years ago, just after his arrival in New York, since he had wanted to publish Tinor's clinical tests as the Materia medica according to MùMille.

Tinor placed his hat and coat on a chair and approached the lectern. When in the lecture hall silence set in, he scratched his lofty brow with his right hand and began his lecture in English, in an unmistakeably Italian accent.

The homoeopathist had no sort of written records which he would have been able to consult during his lecture – even at over eighty years old he did not need them, since his mind was like an inexhaustible source which had stored all the available knowledge and information about homeopathy:

Ladies and Gentlemen,

Thank-you for your attention. Today I do not want to speak about Hahnemann's work, the period of his work and his superb services to homeopathy, which you are indeed all too aware of. No, today I want to discuss the spirit of Hahnemann – how was it possible for him to accomplish something so great?

How was it possible for him to consistently go his own way, even though he faced many obstacles – the jealousy of his colleagues, persecution by the pharmaceutical companies and a total of twelve children whose hungry mouths he had to feed? Indeed, there was nothing which could dissuade Hahnemann from his deep conviction! These people who get their teeth into a set idea are called fantasists or deadbeats. I say to you – the path may still be difficult – always hold on to your visions, since it is only visionaries who can change the world.

Only the person who has given their word, their idea, and who sticks to this, it is only they who can make the new a reality.

The law of similarities discovered by Hahnemann – "Similia similibus curentur" - was to him not just a spiritual law for healing, indeed, it was so much more; it was the archetypcal divine phenomenon. Hahnemann also saw the simile in bread and wine. Are the body and blood of Christ none other than an ad infinitum potentiated saviour? He made man in order to make a similitude of himself and he gave you wine and bread so you would be similar to him! It could even be said – homeopathy was the beginning ... but more on that another time.

Let's stick to Hahnemann's life. To begin with he didn't know how the law of similarities would work; he only knew that it did work! And Hahnemann did his utmost, indeed he gave his own life over to researching the healing secret of the law of similarities. He made a great deal of sacrifices, to pursue his dedication, to the mercy of knowledge.

And I say to all of you who are gathered here today, you, who still feel the power of youth within you - allow nothing and no-one to lead you astray. Your path is the goal – and as you all know, homeopathy is a passion for life.

There are many Hahnemann devotees, who sink their teeth meticulously to his every word and who do not wish to see the bigger picture. Even the homeopathic pontiff of the 20th century Georgos Vithoulkhas warned about novel ideas and theories in homeopathy in posing the question "how far can we go?" But I say to you, thinking outside the box there are so many new things to discover – Hahnemann was only the beginning!

Thank-you all.

Buona sera.

Tinor modestly accepted the applause of the students with a brief nod. They clapped and stamped their feet and wanted to hear more from him, but the old homoeopathist lifted his coat and hat, damp from the rain, and left the lecture gall hastily with small, swift steps.

Tinor hurried to the end of the long corridor and knocked at the door of the office of the Director of the Homeopathic University.

"Good evening Dr. MùMille, please come in, I have been wanting to speak with you for days, but have been unable to reach you on the phone", said Nikola Milec and motioned Tinor to take a seat on the chair opposite his desk. Tinor had taken off his hat, but he kept his coat on as he sat down, to indicate straight away that he had little time today to spend chatting with a colleague.

"Unfortunately I do not have good news. My daughter, as you know, is at the same college as Sarah, the daughter of Samuel Hackman, Health Advisor for the city of New York; a few days ago at a private dinner party I had the opportunity to get chatting to her father in person. He is by the way a very nice, open-minded person – you wouldn't think that about a politician – and over a glass of Champagne I told him about your idea of a homeopathic clinic. As you might imagine he was none too keen on the idea, since that would also mean a considerable financial outlay for the city of New York."

Tinor accepted this news calmly and just nodded in silence.

"But, all is not lost, don't make a face like that! Since Sarah was cured of her considerable allergy by your method of homeopathic pulsation, Samuel is very keen on us and does of course have a sympathetic ear for our healing system", continued Nikola Milec, tapping his ballpoint pen nervously on his desk.

"Nikola, seriously, do you actually see any chance at all for our plan?", asked Tinor, who actually wanted to finish the conversation.

"Tinor, we have known one another for many years. You must have noticed by now that I never give up! Do you think I would have come so far otherwise? At any rate, I have made this, the only homeopathic university in the world, the great place it is today. When I came here as a little country doctor from Croatia and started as a lecturer in an old New Yorker townhouse, I would never have dreamt what importance our university would gain some day! And now we have a first-rate university building. All the famous, contemporary homoeopathists have all lectured here! In the first instance I think that you are the gem among all the homoeopathists; the genius of Hahnemann really is alive in you. I sense Hahnemann's legacy in you!"

Tinor glanced at the door and would have preferred to go but he didn't want to end Nikolas' torrent of words with an impolite remark.

"I was able to scoop you", continued Milec and drew a deep breath again, "You hold regular lectures here in front of a very large audience; once or twice a week. We have had guest lecturers, of high standing and name, from all over the world! So why shouldn't I succeed in founding a clinic, a homeopathic hospital, which is affiliated to our university?"

"A clinic is another dimension, its gobbles up money running into billions", replied Tinor.

"True. But I'll tell you something, next Tuesday evening I have a private appointment with Samuel Hackman, in his home office! Just for this project! I will prepare myself well for it this week, by drawing up a complete market analysis and an account costing. Then I'll bring your research results on homeopathic pulsation to Samuel. That has to convince him. What do you think now?"

"I congratulate you, Nikola, but you do know me. I won't break into a paroxysm of joy prematurely. We'll wait and see what the discussion yields, then we can be happy."

Without waiting for an answer from Dr. Milec, Tinor got up, put on his hat and extended his hand to Nikola across the desk.

"O.k., Professor, we'll meet in a few days at your next lecture. Should I hear anything more before then I will of course let you know straight away!"

Tinor took his leave at the door again with a silent nod.

"Are you well?", Nikola also enquired, "You seem somehow different today? I know that small talk is not your strong point but you are indeed a person who lives on visions, at least that is what you preach."

"Yes, everything is great; I am just getting on with my studies, which is why I have to get back home urgently to finish my notes. But thank you for asking; I am well."

"O.k. then, happy creating!"

Tinor hurried to leave the university. Before he went home however he made a brief detour to the New York Memorial Hospital. After around half an hour he left the hospital and then hurriedly made his way back home again.

Chapter 25

"For such experiments – on which depend the certainty of the complete art of healing and the welfare of all the generations of people to co me –I believe, no other medicines should be employed than those which we know fully about, and of whose purity, authenticity and full effectiveness are fully assured."

Samuel Hahnemann

Tinor unlocked his apartment, hung his coat, wet through from the rain, on the peg, slipped into his felt slippers and got immediately to work. He took one test tube after another out of the wooden rack, shook each carefully, held it to the light and examined it for a long time. Finally he nodded silently as though an inner vision had revealed to him which would be the right one; the homoeopathist had made his choice.

Using a pipette Tinor removed a droplet of blood from this test tube, pumped it into a vial and filled it with 99 drops of a mixture of alcohol and water. Thin, light pink streaks of blood now infused through the translucent liquid. The old man closed the vial with a rubber stopper and put it on the old sideboard which served as laboratory equipment.

He looked at his work satisfied. He then lifted this vial again and gave it 100 vigorous succussions, rapping it on a pigskin bound edition of Samuel Hahnemann's "Organon of Medicine" dating from the year of Tinor's birth 1921.

He then wrote down on a piece of paper:

"MùMille: C 1".

The homoeopathist now took another drop of this dynamised liquid with the pipette, put it in a new vial and added 99 drops of the alcohol-water mixture. He carried a further 100 successions, rapping it on the book, and obtained the next highest potency level, the C 2.

Having attained the C 30, Tinor MùMille paused briefly and looked at his remedy. He calculated the centesimal potency – it was dilution of 1 to a 1 followed by 60 zeros.

Without resting or sleeping, the old man continued unremittingly to potentiate, until the next evening he had achieved a potency level of C 1000.

He proudly examined his end product, which differed neither externally nor chemically from the other potency levels. He then labelled the vial "MùMille C 1000" and carefully put this nosode down on Hahnemann's "Organon of Medicine", which lay as ever on the old sideboard.

Tinor turned on the tap in the kitchen sink, supported his back, hunched with pain, with both his elbows and then held both hands for a long time under the icy cold water to alleviate the swelling and redness from all the succussion.

He then lay down on the sofa to rest, so he could take a final look at his precious remedy before falling into a dreamless sleep, completely exhausted.

Chapter 26

"Don't change the slightest symptom, observe everything. Receive the message undisturbed and get it on paper, there is no other way for a physician to perform his function and do his duty."
James Tyler Kent

When the homoeopathist awoke the next day it was already afternoon, and it was still raining in torrents. Tinor was horrified, since the hour hand on the kitchen had already past four. He had had to resume his series of lectures about Samuel Hahnemann in the Homeopathic University of New York in the morning. Tinor had no time to lose. However he didn't feel it necessary to apologise to the university for his gaffe. He had recently had his telephone cut off, since to him it was merely a disturbance of these modern times.

Contented, he looked again at his nosode, the MùMille C 1000. Tired, he sat on the sofa and smoothed the grey wisps on both sides of his temples behind his ears. He then made some tea, sat down at his bureau and opened a thick book bound in pigskin.

The rain still pelted on the window panes and it was so dull that Tinor had to put on a light to write. The thick buck was almost filled with writing. It was his Materia Medica, which contained all the key self-experiments using homeopathic remedies and many other details from his decades of research. "Hahnemann's Legacy", was the name of his Materia Medica. Only the final three pages remained unwritten. Tinor dipped his quill, a relic from olden times which he held dear, into a small inkpot and began in meticulous fine script with the final chapter heading – "MùMille C 1000".

Without taking a single break, he wrote the final three pages of his work on the beige parchment paper. He ended his notes with the sentence,

"May this knowledge serve to heal all of mankind; that is Hahnemann's Legacy!"

Tinor wanted to continue working. But as he took a brief rest on the sofa again, he dozed off and dreamed about his little sister Lucia. When he came round again, he was dazed, and suddenly felt too old and powerless to complete his work. He wanted to sit up but couldn't manage it. The memory of Lucia had upset him too much; too great was the knowledge that in this life he had found love for but brief moments. His eyes moistened and he thought about those wonderful moments in Amsterdam, about Frederike, that tender, angel-like being, who he had been able to hold in his arms for so few moments.

Slowly Tinor managed to straighten himself up. Everything was in a spin; this dizziness did not want to end and he had to steady himself with both hands on the sofa. The homoeopathist was tired of life, after a considerable time he felt that his time would soon be up. Exhausted, he lay on the back of the chair, let his head tilt back, and in a haze of semi-sleep various images of his life cropped up in his mind, as if he had to bid farewell to each of them, before he could go over to a whole other reality.

He thought about how it had been that it was almost

60 years ago that he had last seen his sister Lucia. At the time when he upon finishing his homeopathy studies visited Resina, before travelling to Roderick in Amsterdam. And when Tinor once again awoke from this semi-conscious state, he was overcome by a great melancholy. Sluggishly he got up from the sofa and stumbled to the cupboard, took out the farewell letter from his little sister Lucia from an old, dusty box and read it one last time.

Weary, Tinor then tried to rid himself of the painful memories and to immerse himself in the here and now again. Veratrum album now was his simile, a homeopathic emergency remedy, which now helped him to overcome the coldness within him and stabilise his circulation. After this administration his sorrow about his little sister vanished, in the knowledge that he would soon see Lucia in another world.

The homoeopathist now prepared himself with newly found inner serenity to complete his last work on earth; an act of the utmost love, indeed a gift to all humanity! Amore sempre c'è! He wanted to finally prove to people that he too could love.

And with the thought that a person might perhaps have but one passion in life, the homoeopathist got back to work, refreshed and now almost happy.

He read through his last notes about MùMille C 1000 with deep satisfaction and closed "*Hahnemann's Legacy*".

He then shuffled into the corridor, put on his outdoor shoes and slipped on his coat and hat. He had to hurry now and get away before anyone from the university came to enquire about his sudden absence. He had wasted too much time dozing. Tinor went back to the sideboard and took the vial of MùMille C 1000, which was still on the pigskin bound edition of Hahnemann's "Organon of Medicine".

He held the nosode in his left hand and looked at it for a long time again. He then stashed this homeopathic high potency remedy in his jacket pocket, grabbed an old rumpled plastic bag which was lying by the front door and hastily left the apartment.

Chapter 27

"The highest and most effective medicine is love."
Paracelsus

Tinor walked along the rain-sodden avenue and turned right into the long driveway to the main entrance of the New York Memorial Hospital. In the back area of the entrance hall, as well as the many lifts, there were also staff and goods lifts in which nurses transported sickbeds. Lots of people were waiting in front of the lifts, which meant that Tinor was able to slip unnoticed into an empty good lift. He pressed the button for the third basement floor.

Once there, he headed for the staff toilets opposite and shut himself in there. Tinor ditched his coat and hat and put on a white doctor's coat which was in his plastic bag. He then took his nosode and put it in the pocket of the coat.

Tinor's eyes sparkled, and a mischievous smile flashed over his face when he looked at himself in the mirror in the toilet. Like the cat that got the cream, he smoothed what grey strands of hair he had left behind his ears, nodded to himself and then opened the toilet door slightly. No-one was to be seen in the long, brightly lit corridor. There was not a sound. Tinor quietly slipped out of the toilets and recalled when as a child he had often tip-toed out of his home. This thought must have made him chuckle to himself.

The old man then turned left into a corridor and followed the signposts which showed the way to the hospital archives and to the goods store for the radiological department. Tinor then took the next corridor on the right which now looked quite different to the other corridors. He had now reached the old building of the New York Memorial Hospital, whose walls were unrendered. It smelt of musty dampness and the dark lighting seemed to be from the 1920s. Tinor proceeded along the long, narrow corridor until he reached a door which had "Access to authorised personnel only" written on it.

He carefully pushed down the handle and the door opened automatically. It had worked. For the last few days Tinor had sawn the lock. No-one had been there in the interim and noticed that the lock had been tampered with, no-one realised that the door was no longer locked.

In front of Tinor was the water reservoir for the New York Memorial Hospital. In a giant underground collecting tank, hundreds of thousands of litres of drinking lay before him, which ensured the giant hospital complex had a supply of water, even in times of emergency of catastrophe.

With something approaching celebration, Tinor now looked at the tank and listened to the loud, monotone rushing of the water which was constantly flowing in through the water system.

With a ceremonial gesture, Tinor then took the vial with the MùMille C 1000 out of his jacket pocket.

"Similia similibus curentur", he chuckled, giving an approving nod again and with a soft pop of the plastic cap, opened the vial of homeopathic remedy. He then trickled the entire contents of the MùMille C 1000 into the drinking water reservoir of the New York Memorial

Hospital.

Tinor chuckled again to himself; it was almost as if his chuckling had now become hysterical laughter, like Rumpelstiltskin, the little creature who hopped around a fire on one leg singing, "It's great that no-one knows..."

Chapter 28

"Ah, there the learned man I recognize!
What you touch not, in furthest distance lies,
What you grasp not, must simply be untrue,
What you count not, you fancy is unreal,
What you weigh not, lacks any weight for you,
What you coin not, will never pass, you feel."
Johann Wolfgang von Goethe

When a few days later the door to Tinor's apartment was forced at the behest of Nikola Milec, they found Dr. MùMille dead on his sofa. An enlightened smile was on his rigid lips and his eyes, looking up to heaven, showed that he had not struggled in death, rather, the homoeopathist must have gone to sleep in a sort of spiritual rapture.

Nonetheless, the New York police did not rule out suicide since everything indicated that the death of the old man had not occurred suddenly - his apartment was spick and span, there was also no left-over food, and the bin had been emptied. The police were unable to determine any signs of trauma; on account of the considerable age of the deceased, a post-mortem was ruled out.

The only useable legacy was found beside the dead man, a book - „Hahnemann's Heritage". It contained the deceased's personal research findings and descriptions of remedies, the Materia Medica of MùMille. However, the last described MùMille C 1000 was never found amongst his homeopathic items.

Tinor's student Hans Ganter was the only one to

whom he left anything. In an envelope, MùMille had bequeathed to him his gold wrist watch with Hahnemann's law "Similia similibus curentur" engraved on it. He had also written a few personal lines:

"Dear Ganter, I am bequeathing Hahnemann's Legacy to you. See to the simile principle and you too will be a shadow healer for all of mankind. With heartfelt thanks, Tinor"

To all his other students he bequeathed a handwritten message which he simply wrote on a slip of paper and placed on Hahnemann's Organon of Medicine on the kitchen dresser. The message read:

"Amore sempre c'é."

EPILOGUE

Since my early retirement, I have sat alone in my work room every evening, have taken out "Hahnemann's Legacy" and read the final three pages of Tinor's handwritten notes about MùMille C 1000 for the thousandth time. Yet I have never worked out what happened to this peculiar nosode of his own blood. I don't know what Tinor did with it, how nobody had found it in his apartment and why Tinor even made it.

So to find out what Dr. MùMille meant in his final words, I needed time, a great deal of time.

In many nights of pure despair when I seemed to be as far from MùMille's secret than ever, I sometimes read the bible. Time and again I ardently skimmed through the Book of Revelation – it too seemed to have a secret which I could not reveal. And one evening as I read a certain passage again and again, the scales finally fell from my eyes,

"The third angel sounded his trumpet, and a great star, blazing like a torch, fell from the sky on a third of the rivers and on the springs of water— the name of the star is Bitterness. A third of the waters turned bitter, and many people died from the waters that had become bitter".

And from that second I knew what the simile principle really meant. What terrorists made for evil, can also be used to do good. And I was quite sure - Tinor must have done it before me already. And because I also must have drunk the MùMille C 1000 nosode from the tap water in the hospital, I too have been inspired by MùMille's spirit; his ideas have infected me; I have become more and more similar to him and have finally become his simile...

A completely new idea finally came to me – the potency of MùMille's concept; I would not manufacture any human nosode to heal the world, no, I would create a divine one! This is the task which my tutor Tinor MùMille bequeathed to me.

I will potentiate the Turin Shroud and with this cure I will reveal the divine simile principle to all of mankind. I will pour this godlike cure like a burning torch of love into the rivers and oceans of this world and then, one day, when we have all tasted it, we will finally realise that we too are God's similitude! Amore sempre c'è!

When wars end sometime and people begin to fraternize, when walk hand in hand and we love the next person like we love ourselves – then we will know, the divine simile is working!

Acknowledgements

Good things come to those who wait! I have written Hahnemann's Legacy in stages over a period of ten years; gradually interwoven the plotline and cemented it with medical and medical-historical knowledge. When I went on a fantastic trip to Pompeii and to the Sorrento Coast in the year 2000, the story of Tinor MùMille began to evolve within me. But I suppose the right time to publish it has only come now!

Special thanks go to my editor Lucia Eppelsheim, who squeezed out so much more from my words than I could ever have hoped. To my translator, Lisa Rodgers, who has put her heart and soul into translating my novel into English, I would like to express my praise and thanks. To my graphic designer, Thomas Blaha, who has created such a wonderfully harmonious book cover.

I also extend my thanks to my parents, my son and his father Josef too of course, as well as all my kind friends who often had to be "proofreaders" and who have been so supportive to me in the last ten years! Last, but not least, I would like to thank my lovely cat Pia, just for being there!

Petra Neumayer
April 2014

Petra Neumayer

Single-handed dowsing rod course

Practical guidance for energy testing
using a tensor

Notes for seminars and self-learning course

Skripthaus Verlag

The ideal method for self-help in your everyday life as
well for therapy and healing: learn the simple art of
how to use a single-handed dowsing rod. Nerve and
muscle impulses transfer the right answers to our
questions through the tensor. Our intuition is made
visible through the deflections of the tensor. This
therapy is based on the principles of the "New
Homeopathy".

Skripthaus Verlag ISBN-13: 978-1495973178

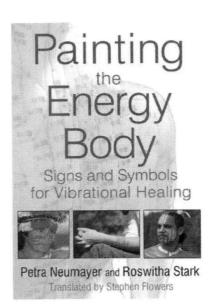

Painting
the
Energy
Body
Signs and Symbols
for Vibrational Healing

Petra Neumayer and Roswitha Stark
Translated by Stephen Flowers

Geometric symbols and signs have been drawn on
the body to enhance strength and courage and
stimulate the body's powers of self-healing since
prehistoric times - the most ancient evidence being
the 5,000-year-old iceman "Otzi," found in the Alps
in 1991 who had symbols tattooed over his arthritic
joints. Found in indigenous societies around the
globe, symbols on the body - whether drawn,
painted or tattooed - act as energy antennae,
triggering healing impulses in the energy body and
meridian system. The authors illustrate the key
symbols used in this practice and reveal how to
select the proper symbol for your condition.

Inner Traditions ISBN-13: 978-1594774805

Printed in Great Britain
by Amazon